JAILBREAKS:

99 CANADIAN SONNETS

T0161443

JAILBREAKS:

99 CANADIAN SONNETS

EDITED BY

ZACHARIAH WELLS

BIBLIOASIS

FIRST EDITION

Library and Archives Canada Cataloguing in Publication

Wells, Zachariah, 1976-
    Jailbreaks : 99 Canadian sonnets / Zachariah Wells.

ISBN 13: 978-1-897231-44-9
ISBN 10: 1-897231-44-X

    1. Sonnets, Canadian (English). I. Title.
PS8645.E458J332008 C811'.04208 C2008-900202-4

 Canada Council Conseil des Arts
for the Arts du Canada

 ONTARIO ARTS COUNCIL
CONSEIL DES ARTS DE L'ONTARIO

We gratefully acknowledge the support of the Canada Council for the Arts and the Ontario Arts Council for our publishing program.

PRINTED AND BOUND IN CANADA

JAILBREAKS:
99 CANADIAN SONNETS

Contents

EDITOR'S INTRODUCTION

I lifted the title for this book – the first of its kind to appear in Canada since Lawrence Burpee's *A Century of Canadian Sonnets* in 1910 – from Margaret Avison's unparaphrasable sonnet "Snow," which begins "Nobody stuffs the world in at your eyes. / The optic heart must venture: a jail-break / And re-creation." This struck me as the perfect encapsulation of the work gathered in this anthology and an apt metaphor for the delightful lessons the collection as a whole contains.

First, there's the sonnet itself, whose history is that of a form refusing to be contained within a narrow cell, proving itself adept at daring escapes and covert crossings. Far more than other forms, it has been defined by its adaptability, flexibility, plasticity. Its deceptively ample cargo space can accommodate – and has done so – pithy wit and irony, intellectual investigations and expressions of sincere feeling. A good poet can take liberties – often outrageous ones – with a sonnet's structure without destroying the sonnet's essence.

Don Paterson has said that the sonnet "represents one of the most characteristic shapes human thought can take." Sonnets are built the way that people think and speak and argue. The sonnet's stability underlines the basic unity of human experience and identity, even while its mutations reflect the emergence of new idioms and worldviews. From its origins in 13th century Italy as a conventional love poem, to Wyatt and Surrey's 16th century importations and adaptations, to Spenser's reconfiguration of rhyme-scheme, to Shakespeare's honing of Surrey's English form, to Milton's single-breath rush and caudated variants, to John Clare's homely supplets (to borrow Seamus Heaney's apposite coinage), to Hopkins' ten-and-a-half line curtal, a wild twenty-four line caudate and his sprung-rhythm experiments with more "normal" sonnets, to George Meredith and Tony Harrison's sixteen-line variants, to Auden and Lowell's unrhymed sonnets and Paul Muldoon's ludic play with rhyme and line-length, the form has gone through more twists and contortions – not to mention permutations in diction and subject matter, both subtle and radical – than can be enumerated here. As Richard Sanger, a contributor to this volume, has said, "The great virtue of the sonnet in English is in how, mirroring history and the heart, it has admitted and contained such disruption, which it has often sung as a sweet disorder or sudden blow, remaining, like Wyatt's muse, 'wild for to hold though I seem tame.'"

The canny sonneteers I've corralled in this book – an exercise akin to the proverbial herding of cats – have learned and profited from the sonnet's erratic orbits. Though some of the poems I've selected are more or less orthodox in structure and subject, most are not. The critically-minded reader will search this volume in vain for lines composed to an iambic metronome's beat, padded with extraneous verbiage and syntactic distortions; for the sentimental treatment of conventional themes; for reactionary neo-Georgian gentilities. These sonneteers know that it takes just as much inventive innovation and rigorous vigor to write a good sonnet as it does to create a new form. More, in fact, since superficial novelty is often a disguise for banality and ineptitude. For these sonneteers, Pound's clarion call to "make it new" has not gone unheeded, but has been interrogated forcefully in order to determine just what "it" is that must be made fresh. They understand that innovation doesn't come from thin air, but must be founded on the bedrock of poetry's traditions. For them, innovation involves not tearing down brick and timber buildings and erecting steel and concrete edifices in their place, but the intelligent and conscientious renovation of sound frames already standing, retrofitting old homes to serve contemporary tastes and needs, surviving what Don Coles calls in his contribution to this book "the catastrophe of time."

Contrary to what one might think about Canadian poetry, the sonnet never went away. It did go underground for a while, which is part of the reason that some of the poems and poets in this book haven't received the kind of recognition they deserve. But now many younger poets, not content to repeat the procedures of their poetic forebears, are hungry for change. It's getting hard to open a journal or a new collection without stumbling over some sort of sonnet, or even a book-length sequence of them. Today's poets have no insecurity about looking abroad and into the past for inspiration and instruction. They understand that the greatest glory of Canadian identity is its prismatic variety. Something that strikes me, looking at the roster I've assembled, is the sheer number of immigrants and emigrants peopling this anthology – border-crossing poets who can't be confined to the national or regional boxes we tend to put them in. This is reflected by the formal variety of the poems and it says a great deal, I think, about the portmanteau portability and cosmopolitaneity of the sonnet, a poetic form whose protean history is a (sometimes) gentle rebuke to hidebound provincialism. The poets in this book have launched their sturdy sonnet craft and sailed them, in Fred Cogswell's phrase, "to wider regions where the river goes." I invite you now to follow.

Zachariah Wells
New Westminster
January 7, 2008

THE TALISMAN

I carry for my safety
an unimportant stone,
not smooth to touch, not lovely,
but quite my own.
It's not sharp or heavy,
but useless in my hand—
significant of nothing,
a stone I understand.

Until this nothing fails me
I'm safe, as safe as stone,
but once I give it meaning, art
will give the meaningless a heart,
and heart is nothing safe in hand,
and nothing I can understand.

David W. McFadden

COUNTRY HOTEL IN THE NIAGARA PENINSULA

The guy was shooting pool. I stopped to watch.
He missed an easy shot and the cue ball
hopped the cushion and crashed to the floor.
"I'm bad luck," I murmured apologetically
as I scurried to the door. "You sure are,"
the guy yelled after me, his voice melting
into the evening fog, streaked with light from the
streetlamps and the headlights of cars on Highway 8.

Everybody understands my poetry. There is nothing
hidden. A large mind examines a small mind,
mounts it like a butterfly, splits it open
under intense light, an ongoing autopsy
in the morgue of all our lives.
You know everything you need to know.

Don Coles

SAMPLING FROM A DIALOGUE

Stopping by the bedroom wall he says God
damn it Marge (if that's her name), we have been through
this forty thousand times now let's have a new
line, I need to hear something different, and this odd
and, well, obviously inflated, analogy comes into his mind
—Roland, at Roncesvalles, and *his* last long call—
and he stands where he happens to be, beside the wall
and waits, listening, he knows now he's waiting for some kind
of miracle, what's she going to say,
one of them always finds a consoling pose
and his feel all used up, and he tries to picture those
horsemen, bright lances, rescuing armies on the way,
and from the bed behind him she says *Well*
maybe there is just such a thing as
having enough of somebody,
breaking the rhyme,
and both of them stay where they are, too far
apart again, in a clarity neither of them expected or thought
they were making, and listen to
the catastrophe of time.

Don McKay

STRESS, SHEAR, AND STRAIN
THEORIES OF FAILURE

They have never heard of lift
and are—for no one, over and over—cleft. Riven,
recrystallized. Ruined again. The earth-engine
driving itself through death after death. Strike/slip,
thrust, and the fault called normal, which occurs
when two plates separate.
Do they hearken unto Orpheus, whose song
is said to make them move? Sure.
This sonnet hereby sings that San Fran-
cisco and L.A. shall, thanks to its chthonic shear,
lie cheek by jowl in thirty million
years. Count on it, mortals. Meanwhile,
may stress shear strain attend us. Let us fail
in all the styles established by our lithosphere.

Michael Parr

PALIMPSEST

If I could grasp a sorrow as it slides
obscene and green into the body's holes
and pick the bone's contention as it hauls
five pins of feeling through the body's slats,
I would be rid of grief and all those sluts
that pock the flesh and set me by the heels,
if I could hold a hell's voice as it hails
weathers and wind through all the body's slits.

But I am man caught in the acts of flesh
whose lad of words leaps in the dying man
and grasping fingers hold the will to flash
in heaven's goodness for the sake of men
and time's enough for all that can be felt
if I could catch these instant wits of mine.

Margaret Avison

SNOW

Nobody stuffs the world in at your eyes.
The optic heart must venture: a jail-break
And re-creation. Sedges and wild rice
Chase rivery pewter. The astonished cinders quake
With rhizomes. All ways through the electric air
Trundle candy-bright disks; they are desolate
Toys if the soul's gates seal, and cannot bear,
Must shudder under, creation's unseen freight.
But soft, there is snow's legend: colour of mourning
Along the yellow Yangtze where the wheel
Spins an indifferent stasis that's death's warning.
Asters of tumbled quietness reveal
Their petals. Suffering this starry blur
The rest may ring your change, sad listener.

Stuart Ross

THE CHILDREN OF MARY
CRAWL BACK AT NIGHT

Jesus, Mary! You've got kids!
I hear them screaming through
your apartment, I see their
toys, they look at me with
dark, dark eyes. Mary, they are
miniature people, smaller than
real ones, and they came out of
your belly. At night, when you
sleep, they crawl back in,
and there they take shelter
against the ugly things—the
cruel neighbours, the exhaust-stained snow.
And you, too, are exhausted, and so am I.
I throw a mirror in the street and try to fly.

Eric Ormsby

CHILDHOOD PIETIES

I grew up sullen, nervous, full of tricks.
St. Paul and Milton were familiar ghosts.
I sniffed First Disobedience from the bricks
And mildewed plaster of the Lord of Hosts;
From smiling lies rouged with a crucifix;
The naphtha'd parlour and the Sabbath roasts;
The bitter bibles where the saved would mix
Apocalyptic gossip with their boasts.

I smirked rebellion and wet my bed.
Even the luster of their sheets was fraud.
At nightmare time their Saviour, leeched with sin,
Crept in beside me, worming through my head,
Embraced me, stroked me, kissed me while I clawed
The frogcold mouth of Jesus on my skin.

Christopher Wiseman

DEPARTURE GATE

My son expects a sonnet in this book,
He tells me, grinning, as we shake hands. I
Say I don't have one planned, then catch a look
Of my father's face in his—the mouth, the eye—

And watch him stride away, through the big door
Where I can't follow. Oh son, at twenty-four
You don't know how important farewells are,
Or how they bring back things too hard too bear,

Grim things from which we think we can't recover.
Fly safely. I'll write, I promise. I turn away,
Remembering how it was to be that young

And things were always waiting, journeys over,
Not left behind, the way it feels today.
(Dad, since you died each day is tilted wrong.)

George Johnston

CATHLEEN SWEEPING

The wind blows, and with a little broom
She sweeps against the cold clumsy sky.
She's three years old. What an enormous room
The world is that she sweeps, making fly
A little busy dust! And here am I
Watching her through the window in the gloom
Of this disconsolate spring morning, my
Thoughts as small and busy as her broom.

Do I believe in her? I cannot quite.
Beauty is more than my belief will bear.
I've had to borrow what I think is true:
Nothing stays put until I think it through.
Yet, watching her with her broom in the dark air,
I give it up. Why should I doubt delight?

Amanda Jernigan

LULLABY

My little lack-of-light, my swaddled soul,
December baby. Hush, for it is dark,
and will grow darker still. We must embark
directly. Bring an orange as the toll
for Charon: he will be our gondolier.
Upon the shore, the season pans for light,
and solstice fish, their eyes gone milky white,
come bearing riches for the dying year:
solstitial kingdom. It is yours, the mime
of branches and the drift of snow. With shaking
hands, Persephone, the winter's wife,
will tender you a gift. Born in a time
of darkness, you will learn the trick of making.
You shall make your consolation all your life.

Diana Brebner

WHAT IS HOMELESS IN ME, AND SIGHTLESS

What is homeless in me, and sightless, not
without love, but blind to your world? If I

insist on love, or sight, something not brought
by insisting, who will still cherish my

eyes, kiss them with tenderness, with darkness?
All of those places within me, somewhat

lonely, and foreign, where I am homeless,
still remain to be seen. The terror that

fills me is one dark place. The fear of sight
is another. I would like to believe

love is blind; blindness is something to fight
for, to believe in. Dear man, when I leave

my eyes open, I see nothing, in this
world we call real, but you: you and darkness.

David Solway

from "POSTCARDS FROM PLATI YALOS"

I'm writing this because I'm desperate.
I know that you're familiar with my fits,
that you're tired and skeptical, but habit
compels me, and I have no intimates
to talk my madness out with. I write this
as if it were a meditated note
(distilled from years of island loneliness)
I slipped into a flask and set afloat
to cross the waste of wine-dark memory,
that commonplace, unHomeric, barren,
sentimental stretch of personal sea.
What the note says is, I love you, Karin.
Forgive me all the cards that I have sent
but the days go by as if they didn't.

Sharon McCartney

IMPENDING DEATH OF THE CAT

Something's wrong with the cat, scarecrow—she wanes
gossamer thin, ghostly, her spine a prominent
span, a Golden Gate, from which her mane
of dandruffed fur hangs. Hundreds at the vet,
blood tests, scans, potassium, kidney, all
normal. Is she just old? Pampered, she persists,
but for how long? I plump a challis shawl—
soft wool, her stately sickbed—buy Fancy Feast,
patiently sop the hazards of vomit, clean
the quilt *ad nauseum*, try to ignore
the debris of death, messiness, futile routine
of food and shit. Say it: nothing will restore
her health. And yet, remark her purr, her carriage,
how capably she embodies the state of our marriage.

Mike Barnes

FIRST STAB

Something is off in you, she said,
and, happy it wasn't *she* half-dead,
she based her kisses on it.
Body over mind responded
(at seventeen no great contest)
and from Valentine's till harvest
we flew to the lust part faster
when we realized what a vaster
illness, like mental leprosy,
was rotting the limbs and lips we
could still unironically call blessed
as hotly they, as we, caressed.
A better one could cure this stuff,
whispered a voice, dismissing love.

J.D. Black

ANTIHEROIC COUPLETS

"Most of that war I worked a rifle range—
Boot camp instructor; saw the sorry change
From volunteers to draftees. Some weak-guts
SOBs thought they'd save their sad-sack butts,
Giving that combat infantryman's badge
A miss by failing riflery. I'd cadge
A spot near centre range each time we had
A qualifying shoot. My eyes weren't bad
Back then: if someone left his target blank
I'd put some rounds in for him—you could bank
On me for bulls and inners. Had some fun
Then: thought I was a real son of a gun.
But why do I remember most those scared
Young bastards' faces, staring, stunned by what they'd
      scored?"

Goran Simić

I WAS A FOOL

I was a fool to guard my family house in vain
watching over the hill somebody else's house shine,
and, screaming, die in flames. I felt no sorrow and no pain
until I saw the torches coming. The next house will be mine.

If I wasn't somebody else, as all my life I've been,
I wouldn't say to my neighbour that I feel perfectly fine
upon seeing his beaten body. I should offer my own skin
as a tarp. Will the next beaten body be mine?

I was a fool. I love this sentence. Long live Goran and his sin.
There is no house or beaten man. There is no poetry, no line,
there is no war, there are no neighbours. There's no tarp made
    of skin.
But there's a pain in my stomach as I write this. It's only mine,

this sentence, the one I swallowed, whose every word
is each of the flames I saw, every scream a sword.

Ralph Gustafson

"S.S.R., LOST AT SEA." *—THE TIMES.*

What heave of grapnels will resurrect the fabric
Of him, oceans drag, whereof he died,
Drowning sheer fathoms down, liquid to grab on—
Sucked by the liner, violence in her side?
Of no more sorrow than a mottled Grief
In marble. There fantastic in the murk,
Where saltwhite solitary forests leaf,
He swings: the dark anonymously works.
For who shall count the countless hands and limbs
In ditch and wall and wave, dead, dead
In Europe: touch with anguished name and claim
And actual tear, what must be generally said?
O let the heart's tough riggings salvage him,
Only whose lengths can grapple with these dead.

S.S. Athenia
September 3, 1939

E.J. Pratt

THE GROUND SWELL

Three times we heard it calling with a low,
   Insistent note; at ebb-tide on the noon;
   And at the hour of dusk, when the red moon
Was rising and the tide was on the flow;
Then, at the hour of midnight once again,
   Though we had entered in and shut the door
   And drawn the blinds, it crept up from the shore
And smote upon a bedroom window-pane;
Then passed away as some dull pang that grew
   Out of the void before Eternity
   Had fashioned out an edge for human grief;
Before the winds of God had learned to strew
His harvest-sweepings on a winter sea
   To feed the primal hungers of a reef.

Anita Lahey

from "CAPE BRETON RELATIVE"

*In Which Your Uncle Recalls the Last Time He Traversed
the Treacherous Tittle on the Way to Scaterie*

"Twelve, I was, and after duck. The boat
a dropped ladle, dipping, rolling, old George
steering, old George drunk, one-legged George:
his gun, his whiskey, his dog and full throat
of smoke against the froth, the belch: the tittle
versus the hull. The day was yellow, mean.
At George's boots a can of gasoline,
puncture in its side: a greasy dribble.

"Imagine. Sure we landed, hunted. Fire
in my dreams? I don't suppose. I plucked
my dinner, dear. I guess you might admire
me for that." Old George, old times, old luck.
Your uncle laughs and veers toward the rock.
Your uncle drinks; the bottom splashes higher.

Kenneth Leslie

from "BY STUBBORN STARS"

The silver herring throbbed thick in my seine,
silver of life, life's silver sheen of glory;
my hands, cut with the cold, hurt with the pain
of hauling the net, pulled the heavy dory,
heavy with life, low in the water, deep
plunged to the gunwale's lips in the stress of rowing,
the pulse of rowing that puts the world to sleep,
world within world endlessly ebbing, flowing.
At length you stood on the landing and you cried,
with quick low cries you timed me stroke on stroke
as I steadily won my way with the fulling tide
and crossed the threshold where the last wave broke
and coasted over the step of water and threw
straight through the air my mooring line to you.

Brenda Tate

THE LAST MATE

Across the water we watched the starspackle spit
of guns that grunted and coughed over pitch and swell
from a darkened barque that juddered and swung and fell;
when our deck blew off, I arrowed the air on a sprit.
Slicker than tar, an unbreakable storm cascade
flung over our rolling bones as a score were trapped
by wave wrack, sucked under sail, their foreheads wrapped
with seaweed crowns, their cruciate legs outsplayed.

Then the ocean rose to hills we could not climb
and our new dead rippled like ribbons over the crests
with frozen bows of hands on abandoned breasts,
while undines prisoned their souls in coats of rime.
Washed naked but safe, I grappled a better rest
than the white salt-men made gods before their time.

Charles Bruce

EARLY MORNING LANDING

In daylight, there is life and living speech;
The constant grumble, the resilient splash
Of slow tide lifting on a slanted beach;
And blowing sunlight. And the measured flash
Of the sea marching . . . But the beach and bay
Are vague as midnight now; in midnight thinned
At the sky's edge by the first hint of grey.
And calm as sleep before the morning wind.

Calmer than sleep. But the eyes lift to find
In the veiled night the faint recurring spark
Of a known beacon. And the listening mind
Wakes in the stillness; and the veil is stirred
By a dim ghost of sound—a far-off word
And the soft thump of rowlocks in the dark.

Steven Price

from *Anatomy of Keys*

XVI

                    Rope:
            sleek sash cord, escapologist's skin,
                umbilical of the drowned, woven shroud
hanged men bladder and drag and stretch out in;
wildfire ripple of rumour through a crowd;
sheath, frayed bloodline, sinew of fire and flint:
                asleep in one's lap like a child or a cat
and like a child all ululation, all wailed lament;
rope like a brambled path, leading both in and out;
                elbow; cut tongue; black intestine or spleen:
                dark many-cornered flesh a knot can be.
A kind of thread and weft we work behind,
what binds us and unbinds us, God to man:
Holy of Holies, spell, hand, prayer, shine:
                the shaking of my father's hands in mine.

Carmine Starnino

ROPE HUSBANDRY

Lark's Head, Cat's Paw, Monkey's Fist, Constrictor.
I've mastered each. I can show you, step by step,
a Flemish Eye, a Granny. But if you ever come back
I'll start with a True Lover. Its breaking strength
(dare I say it?) is very low. Or better yet, the Thief:
capable of holding a large load (the fleeing bandit,
no doubt) but confuse the wrong end of the rope
and its quick release can be disastrous. I think your
favourite would be the Wagoner's Hitch, a method
that bowses down fast on an object but secures
a temporary purchase, and can therefore be easily
undone. I'd rather offer you a simple, well-made
knot, nothing too fancy, one that grips very tightly
and stays tied. Hangman, Strangle, Shroud laid.

John Barton

SAINT JOSEPH'S HOSPITAL, 1937

My heart, a knot undone with pain, forgot
a beat, the message cut. I lie awake,
my life in jars of paint. The thirst I slake
with tears is loss, a canvas stretched too taut
by years misspent, the will of God I thought
assuaged and framed. Totemic fir now break
through mist and gulp the dusk in draughts. I shake
with breath. A month of pain has cast my lot.

I lie awake. To live, the Doctor said,
the trees and sky must rest. My pain must rest.
A breeze afire with shades of summers past
now scents my room. Machine aloft my bed
I type them out, neglected coasts so blessed
with myth, the poles I sketched. They hold me fast.

Steven Heighton

MISSING FACT

> Noli me tangere, *for Caesars I ame;*
> *And wylde for to hold, though I seeme tame.*
> —Thomas Wyatt, c. 1535

Sometimes time turns perfect rhyme to slant,
as in Wyatt's famous sonnet—how the couplet
no longer chimes, his "ame" turned "am," now coupled
more by pattern, form. So everything gets bent
and tuned by time's tectonic slippage. You and
I, for instance, no longer click or chord
the sharp way we did, when secretly wired
two decades back (not fifty—but then human
prosody shifts faster); and surely that's best—
half-rhyme better suits the human, and consonance,
not a flawless fit, is mostly what counts
over years. But still, this urge (from the past?
our genes?) to shirk all, for one more perfect-
coupling rhyme: for two again as one pure fact.

Shane Neilson

RURAL GOTHIC

And love as blight or the kind of drought
that kills all green, leaving no work
but to weep and level the scorched stalks
with mortgaged machinery; the weather-beaten
crops that couldn't stand pestilence, frost,
or love turned on itself. As soil erodes
and fronds arrest their growth, the season's lost
and fault is no one's. What's left are debts
that must be borne for another year. I've tried
to touch that man who'd throttle a neck
as he did a cracked drive shaft, his grip belied
by how much he felt each failure, a black
and hardened ruin. Love as negative, in reverse,
but still in terms of violence: a kind of verse.

Fred Cogswell

VALLEY-FOLK

O narrow is the house where we are born,
And narrow are the fields in which we labour,
Fenced in by rails and woods that low hills neighbour
Lest they should spill their crops of hay and corn.
O narrow are the hates with which we thorn
Each other's flesh by gossip of the Grundies,
And narrow are our roads to church on Sundays,
And narrow too the vows of love we've sworn.

But through our fields the Saint John river flows
And mocks the patterned fields that we enclose;
There sometimes pausing in the dusty heat
We stretch cramped backs and lean upon our hoes
To watch a seagull glide with lazy beat
To wider regions where the river goes.

Alden Nowlan

ST. JOHN RIVER

The colour of a bayonet this river
that glitters blue and solid on the page
in tourist folders, yet some thirty towns
use it as a latrine, the sewerage
seeping back to their wells, and farmers maddened
by debt or queer religions winter down
under the ice, the river bottom strewn
with heaps of decomposing bark torn loose
from pulpwood driven south, its acid juice
killing the salmon. August, when the stink
of the corrupted water floats like gas
along these streets, what most astonishes
is that the pictures haven't lied, the real
river is beautiful, as blue as steel.

Geoffrey Cook

from "THE ISLAND" (after Rilke's "DIE INSEL")

The next tide wipes away the muddy shoal,
and everything's the same on every side;
but the little island out there's shut its eyes;
the labyrinthine dykelands have enclosed
the locals, who were born into a sleep
where they mix up many worlds in silence:
for they seldom speak,
their every sentence
an epitaph for flotsam, the unknown
that somehow comes ashore and stays.
And so it is with everything their gaze
takes in from childhood on:
　　　unrelated, unrelenting, and too huge—
　　　a *come-from-away* exaggerating their solitude.

Charles G.D. Roberts

THE POTATO HARVEST

A high bare field, brown from the plough, and borne
    Aslant from sunset; amber wastes of sky
    Washing the ridge; a clamour of crows that fly
In from the wide flats where the spent tides mourn
To yon their rocking roosts in pines wind-torn;
    A line of grey snake-fence, that zigzags by
    A pond and cattle; from the homestead nigh
The long deep summonings of the supper horn.

Black on the ridge, against that lonely flush,
    A cart, and stoop-necked oxen; ranged beside
      Some barrels; and the day-worn harvest-folk,
Here emptying their baskets, jar the hush
    With hollow thunders. Down the dusk hillside
      Lumbers the wain; and day fades out like smoke.

W.W. Campbell

AT EVEN

I sit me moanless in the sombre fields,
The cows come with large udders down the dusk,
One cudless, the other chewing of a husk,
Her eye askance, for that athwart her heels,
Flea-haunted and rib-cavernous, there steals
The yelping farmer-dog. An old hen sits
And blinks her eyes. (Now I must rack my wits
To find a rhyme, while all this landscape reels.)

Yes! I forgot the sky. The stars are out,
There being no clouds; and then the pensive maid!
Of course she comes with tin-pail up the lane.
Mosquitoes hum and June bugs are about.
(That line hath "quality" of loftiest grade.)
And I have eased my soul of its sweet pain.

> —John Pensive Bangs,
>   in the Great Too-Too Magazine for July

David O'Meara

POSTCARD FROM CAMUS

I will be perfectly honest with you:
the heat's just awful. I wander half-dazed
through town, stopping to shake sand from my shoe
while cypresses shimmer in the heat-haze.
At night there's nothing to do except sip
gin and smoke cigarettes with the door shut.
It's too dangerous otherwise—a nip
to the store, that's all. I think I'll go nuts
if something doesn't happen soon. It's hell.
From dawn to dark, we're fixed like specimens
under the sun's searing lamp; I can't tell
up or down, right from left, trapped in its lens.
I only love the brown bodies—young, alert,
and full of joy. Wish you were here.—Albert

George Elliott Clarke

NEGATION

Le nègre negated, meager, *c'est moi*:
Denigrated, negative, a local
Caliban, unlikable and disliked
(Slick black bastard—cannibal—sucking back
Licorice-lusty, fifty-proof whisky),
A rusty-pallor provincial, uncouth
Mouth spitting lies, vomit-lyrics, musty,
Masticated scripture. Her Majesty's
Nasty, Nofaskoshan Negro, I mean
To go out shining instead of tarnished,
To take apart *Poetry* like a heart.
    So my black face must preface your finish,
Deface your *religion*—unerringly,
Unniggardly, like some *film noir* blackguard's.

Daryl Hine

from *Arrondissements*

1er *Palais Royal*

A foreign city in a foreign language:
Errors you will find your way around
Less by misconstruction of an image
Idiomatic as the underground
Than by reference to the lost and found
Out-of-date semantic luggage
And archaic sentimental slang which
Used to mean so much. Beware of the sound,
Volumes of experience rebound,
Sense can take care of itself. Abandoned baggage,
I sought to celebrate you, not confound;
Apart from the smarts you brought me, *grand dommage*,
A throne's stowaway, you still astound
The razor's edge dividing youth from age.

Nancy Holmes

CAN A SONNET BE A JOKE?

Renouncing badly timed, immoral sex
Is difficult to do. She masturbates
And cries and writes, but dreams! They still perplex
Her body, hot with touch that agitates
In that old rhetoric of skin. Can she
Enjamb another line, or chair, or limb?
Can sweet pentameter code a banshee
Wail, or moan, or just a joke for him?
Jokes are best, more fun and far less trouble,
Or so, at least, she *says* when fucking's out.
(How odd a sonnet sounds with that.) This rubble
(Nancy tweaks the beat and mucks about)
Could a finer woman build . . . Oh, stow it—
Lots of fucking makes a better poet.

Irving Layton

SAGEBRUSH CLASSIC

And letting fall, "All life's a gamble,"
I assailed the desert's lush casinos
With craps, blackjack, and even keno.
Swift slung it: civilization is faecal.
So take a flyer. Which I did. Fickle
Or foolish one's luck; though I'd poems to show,
Was tanned-handsome, my movements deft and slow,
Some bunko artist raked my dimes and nickels.
All's shit. Luther protesting from a can,
Down-to-earth dealer dealing twenty-one,
Who clued me into a richer idiom;
Result? I can curse better. Caliban,
Roll those bones. At the end comes fuckface death
—Shows a pair of goose eyes on a green cloth.

E.A. Lacey

from "CANADIAN SONNETS"

We were the land's before the land was ours;
the snow, the rock, the cold—they were all here
waiting their victims, countless thousand years
while we were still unthought, waiting the hour
when Cartier should sail down the shining stream;
and the laws—yes, the laws were also there:
thou shalt not laugh nor drink nor fuck nor swear;
this above all, thou shalt not sing or dream.

They say this was the land God gave to Cain;
it'd take Cain's God to give a land like this,
a God at once of vengeance and of pain,
to whom our shriveled lives are incensed bliss,
who carved his laws upon pre-Cambrian schist,
and stamped that schist into the human brain.

Malcolm Lowry

DELIRIUM IN VERA CRUZ

Where has tenderness gone, he asked the mirror
Of the Biltmore Hotel, cuarto 216. Alas,
Can its reflection lean against the glass
Too, wondering where I have gone, into what horror?
Is that it staring at me now with terror
Behind your frail, tilted barrier? Tenderness
Was here, in this very retreat, in this
Place, its form seen, cries heard by you. What error
Is here? Am I that forked rashed image?
Is this the ghost of love which you reflected?
Now with a background of tequila, stubs, dirty collars,
Sodium perborate, and a scrawled page
To the dead, telephone disconnected?
. . . He smashed all the glass in the room. (Bill:$50)

Colin Carberry

ABATTOIR

The stench of knackered horse carcasses seethes
into noon's flushed stagnant light. Each slow
inescapable death breath blights, impedes,
confuses; hits home with a body blow's
paralyzing insistence, *let me in*.
My one fan whines full tilt, I try to write,
but the sweat sticks, rasps like a second skin.
A stoned sun blanks down on the same old shite.

Blue skies blacken. Somnolent church bells toll.
Coarse hands sort the day's takings in a till.
Our streetlight blinks and goes out. One by one
the furniture store's night screens rattle shut.
A school bus bearing the shades of burnt-out
workers belches past, RUTA: *BABYLON*

Joe Rosenblatt & Catherine Owen

POUNCE

If you touch me you'll feel a surge of rage.
I have this urge to taste your blood, drive
my teeth into the shank of your ogling pity.
You *turistas* shall have no dominion over me.
I'm not your common street waif, I'm housed in pride!
My immaculate ears are the antennae of piety
for when the sun sets I'll bay at my master illumed
inside a burning bush on some sidewalk in Havana.

Ignore my Tudor hide, gristle lines my shadow, Che's
fierce love has sprung my posture. Not even *perros*
escape the virility of the imagination: I'm Cagney,
I'm Brando, I'm Capone! The heat swells my eyeballs
to fruit ripened in alleyways; I crouch over your grave,

Turista, the one the camera carves in your mind.

Pino Coluccio

THE TIME WE WON THE CUP IN '82

Little guys who lug a crooked square
and campanile, and forklift debts,
deal hands and fold out butts,
Bics and joshes at haunts on St. Clair.
They down regrets and coffee swigs and clap
a buddy's back, or grin their big mouth
around a *sangwidge*, here, there, both
at once and nowhere, or nowhere you can map.
But fists and flags and long honks from rusty
Buick boats. Pop tunnels drains.
And TTC's it home at night beat.
But that day we filled the skinny street,
and next day the dailies, like all the dusty
jugs of blood that filled our skinny veins.

Anne Wilkinson

SCHOOL OF HYGIENE

They chisel and they chisel
And they chisel at a word.
They scrub it, they polish it,
They whittle off its skin.
They whittle off its skin
And they whittle off its flesh,
They take the marrow from its bone,
They leave it consciousless.

They put it on a plate,
Garnish it with sprig of thyme,
Aesthetically lean,
Minus vitamins—but clean—
That pallid diners may be fed
On meat that has been ten times bled.

A.J.M. Smith

THE WISDOM OF OLD JELLY ROLL

How all men wrongly death to dignify
Conspire, I tell. Parson, poetaster, pimp,
Each acts or acquiesces. They prettify,
Dress up, deodorize, embellish, primp,
And make a show of Nothing. Ah, but met-
aphysics laughs: she touches, tastes, and smells
—Hence knows—the diamond holes that make a net.
Silence resettled testifies to bells.
'Nothing' depends on 'Thing,' which is or was:
So death makes life or makes life's worth, a worth
Beyond all highfalutin' woes or shows
To publish and confess. 'Cry at the birth,
Rejoice at the death,' old Jelly Roll said,
Being on whisky, ragtime, chicken, and the scriptures fed.

Joshua Trotter

THE TEACHER AND THE PEACH

> "If you weren't bursting," her teacher informed her,
> "you wouldn't need patience."—Philip Roth

The sky holds thunder like a swimmer
gone under holds air, holds the fist
of panic inside the chest, like the first
flush of rapture reined-in, the way grammar
employs the onrush of language,
the way skin holds flesh about to burst
the way lust is engine, all piston and breast
the way a dam yokes the river's surge.
What drives you here? What drags you back
to displace again? What, if you catch it,
pulls you face-forward? What lull, what lack?
Wait don't say it, he says, save it.
I won't touch it—don't need to know.
Be fall fruit, full ripe, and never let go.

Molly Peacock

THE LULL

The possum lay on the tracks fully dead.
I'm the kind of person who stops to look.
It was big and white with flies on its head,
a thick healthy hairless tail, and strong, hooked
nails on its raccoonlike feet. It was a full-
grown possum. It was sturdy and adult.
Only its head was smashed. In the lull
that it took you to look, you took the time to insult
the corpse, the flies, the world, the fact that we were
traipsing in our dress shoes down the railroad tracks.
"That's disgusting." You said that. Dreams, brains, fur,
and guts: what we are. That's my bargain, the Pax
Peacock, with the world. Look hard, life's soft. Life's cache
is flesh, flesh, and flesh.

Stephen Brockwell

THE FRUIT FLY

The veins on the fruit fly's wings map the rivers
of a small corner of Minnesota and Ontario
as they may have flowed or yet may flow.

Out of fruit, out of nothing, the fly beats its wings
a thousand thousand times before hands clap it
not into history, for that would take a scrawl

darker and longer than its 6 point semi-colon
rinsed from the palms, but into diminishing silence.
Let's say the first molecule of air to be unmoved

by its high-pitched harmony marks its end.
By then bananas, mangos and papayas,
pomegranates, quinces and figs, all feared

exotic fruit will burst from their nothings
generations of possible geographies.

George Amabile

POACHED GRILSE

What is the law, out here, where there's no other
boat in sight? We take what we need from the sea
as we've always done, each of us, privately,
and if they won't rise to the bucktail's yellow feather
dancing from sixty yards of line, smothered
in foam, in the sun, for hours, then I'll go deep
with a spinner strung from illicit weights, creeping
through chuck, trolling two slack jigs for cover.

Hauling them in on the wire, half asleep
from the cold, I can see them as rainbows, firm and clean
with the hard shimmer of silver and polished stone.
But there's no sport in this. Chilled to the bone,
I take one more for an old friend who has flown
thousands of miles with a crisp white from the Rhone.

Tim Bowling

PACIFIC SOCKEYE, MOVING EAST

Late October.
The spawner kicks across the border, crosses
below the Rockies, becomes the gushing wound
in the gold flesh of the shot doe, becomes, oh,
becomes the quick shock of fox that clings
like a blinked lash to the corner of my eye
when I walk out in the flakes of snow.
The world is waking to its purity again,
the flesh of the apple recomposing around
the crawling worm of sin. And then I catch
you in my gaze, blush of life, old scale,
soft fur, fruit-bloom—the scarlet strip
of possibility, the flesh of the apple
falling in love with the idea of a skin.

Eric Cole

RIGHT WHALE

We're always leaving, and our young,
enormous mollusks, fasten to our sides.
Their hugs are currents, guidance is the moon
that pulls the girdles of the world. We dive
down into gulfs, long windows, dreams,
not just the swallowed-sailor type, but stretching
from the mud of creatures, necks
and fangs, new fangled, flashing in the air,
for blood's ancestry, forcing toeholds there . . .
and the return, unfisting here to fluke . . .
Air calls the lungs, the nostrils on the head
from each black fathom. Its reluctant dependents
plunge out, unhoisted, our mark upon the earth
is the wallop of old boots on the Atlantic.

Mary Dalton

WINTER COAL

They trotted right up to the foot of the lane,
Cart piled with coal for the light-keeper's shack.
But the cousins said no, no crossing their land—
So they turned round the horse and headed on back
For the boat, loaded her up for the Point.
Jam-packed to the gunnels, she rode low in the water.
A stiff wind from the west and over she went—
Over she toppled, tossed them out in dark water.
One of them got fast to the boat,
Held six hours to the side of her,
His fingernails tore off of him;
His brother's luck broke—
She flipped him in first
And the coal down on top of him.

Patrick Warner

THE TURN

On a steep hill, in a house for one
with a crooked cat and an antique bell,
in the middle of life. This is the place
where you made the turn, having crossed
the line where you could not tell
real from unreal, the climb from years,
wood from your flesh, fur from desire,
that silver bell from your tongue,
which tells the tale of that lonely time
when you thought you were ill,
thought you could not tell unreal
from real, your years from a hill,
self from a house, lust from a cat,
your talk from the sound of a bell.

George Murray

DITCH

How many feet was it in front of my home
that I fell in the ditch that opening night
fifteen years back, drunk and rank of some town
girl's perfume? The bank and weeds' tall theatre

drew a blackout curtain over my prone
form and swayed, a shushed and respectful crowd
viewing a well-known/well-appointed corpse
laid out in the roadside's funeral home.

From a civil bed to the misty primal,
spin me, stars, until I am erect.
Take me by the neck like a mother would, that first
clutch at the nape, lift me to your breast.

Dumb, the cars' searchlights passed my dim cradle.
Dumber still, I lay agape and slept.

Karen Solie

TRUST ME

A drowning dream. Look up. Sunlight snickers
on the swells as fingers trail a calm
and vicious scratch across the surface
of an unsung lake and a boat rocks like a bed,
away. You know there's a town nearby,
but that it's dank and full of felons bent
on some shady holiday. Wake up. The ceiling
is awash with daylight chunnelling through the blinds.

Streetcars ride thin rails across the grid, noise
and indecision at the stops. When to get on. When
to get off. How much time there is to kill
and how much money is enough. Wise up to the rule.
It's fierce, squatting on the track between *yes,
of course I will* and *you fool, you fool.*

A.M. Klein

SENNET FROM GHEEL

And these touched thunders, this delyredrum
Outbrasting boom from shekels of cracked steel
Arrave the whirled goon dapht, as zany in Gheel!
Mad as a hater, come, Nick knows warfrom!
Bedlam, Bicetre, and hundemonium
Are compos and sain compared to the unweal
Of these wildbats that frap in belfrydom!
Or are these horrorbingers we are guerred
And hale in Gheel, and lucid like the rest,
As good and woad as other humus merde?
If so, sweet Lord of Hosts, kind exorcist,
Fling us, un-levined, back to whence we erred,
Zuruck to our lunasylum of the blest.

Colleen Thibaudeau

NOCTURNAL VISIT TO ONE WHO
IS A CHIROPRACTOR BY DAY

The sky is Reckitt's Blue of the bone
And the pavements catch,
For a redbrick house with a deershead
Porched, I watch.
It would have had big windows, curtains of écru lace . . .
And a matching African violet.
On the verandah there a lion (window-box)
Leans head and mane on the topmost pane,
(I fear to rile it.)
Moonlight falls through trees in patches of écru lace . . .
Ah there's the house with the unicorn;
(Voodoo Man, Voodoo Man,
Won't you cure me if you can?)
The Voodoo Man said, Lift the latch.

Gwendolyn MacEwen

THE DISCOVERY

do not imagine that the exploration
ends, that she has yielded all her mystery
or that the map you hold
cancels further discovery

I tell you her uncovering takes years,
takes centuries, and when you find her naked
look again,
admit there is something else you cannot name,
a veil, a coating just above the flesh
which you cannot remove by your mere wish

when you see the land naked, look again
(burn your maps, that is not what I mean),
I mean the moment when it seems most plain
is the moment when you must begin again

John Newlove

GOD BLESS THE BEAR

How many of them die of old age?
They die of the tension of not-knowing,
the apprehension.
                    Fear sits in their guts,
thus the courage, the quickness, the shyness
of a deer asking Are you my death? the gopher
taking one last look. I want to know
what my death looks like
no matter how fast it comes.

Or the bear. God bless the bear,
arthritic as me, doing its death-clown act
on two legs, ready to embrace, saying
I'm just you in funny clothes.
Your clothes are funny too. Let's wrestle,
my little man, my little son, my little death, my brother.

Alan R. Wilson

ORION THE HUNTER

The chair of Women's Studies wrote to the
University administration

On the glut of men as constellations.
After much debate a vast committee

Was created to render gender-free
The universe. Soon sky charts were redone

In ways that cast into oblivion
The cosmic heteropatriarchy.

And yet Orion still rose winter nights.
His bright, expansive rays inflamed parked cars,

Department windows, each roof on campus.
Security then installed blinding lights

So coeds leaving classes after dusk
Would not be taken by that blaze of stars.

Richard Outram

REMEMBRANCE OF BETTY E.

It is certainly one strange kettle of fish, we were all agreed,
sitting around the table, chatting. As if it had all been planned,
the cosmos, it seems, unless it bursts first, is, like some vast
barrage balloon gone bonkers, continuing infinitely to expand;
and then it may, or again it may not, completely collapse back
to a pointless, unthinkably dense mote, incomprehensibly bland;
also, some boffins are starting to talk as if the whole boiling
is a loony tune being played by a one-man band.

And the heat-death of our own insignificant sun is icumin in,
a few tens of millions of years ahead; not a bad one-night stand
for the likes of us zany players, since according to Bishop Ussher
the Creation in every detail occurred in exactly 4004 BC . . . and
as you pointed out (if we hadn't all loved you already, Betty,
we must have forever after!) a half-hour earlier in Newfoundland.

Peter Sanger

FOSSIL FERN

This is the gift of a laminar stain,
an etching of carbon whose
black turns back into green

if you taste it, pinnae
uncoiling, pinnules unfurling
as if they might fly

and flight were one frond away
from this throatful of fern
still growing. A slate of grey

clay is its ground, an earth
you can hold for colour,
shape, speech, all life

in your hands, where spores once
appeared to manipulate silence.

George McWhirter

AN ERA OF EASY MEAT AT LOCARNO

Where I ramble
By Jericho in the March
Mist and murk to take stock,
I glimpse an eagle perched
On a hemlock,
Above a bramble
Patch and rabbit that cannot dissemble
Its giddy nibbles in the grass, a pet bunny
Its bum left to bob like a yoo-hoo to a tummy
In a tree. Fast food, it will tremble
And jerk, then clog the eagle's throat,
Without redress, like a fur
Coat
On a hamburger.

Peter Van Toorn

MOUNTAIN LEAF

A bird pushes a leaf on a red roof,
aiming for ground, so it falls—not the roof,
but the leaf a bird pushes; and the more
it pushes (crisp beak and twig toes), the more
it pushes a still bronze leaf, all curled up
in a cone (showing a beak all curled up
in a cone too, aiming a bronze baked leaf)
for grounds that roll the curls out of a leaf,
grounds which, though rolling round a huger sound,
nevertheless snap twigs in leaf's own sound,
so that, round on round, the red roof, while not
waiting for a leaf to fall, is still not
tongue-tied either, but stands by, push for push,
ready for leafy bird's stiff, crisp, bronze push.

Kevin Connolly

PIANO GAG

the grapes of wrath decant
the leaves of grass derange
the wines of spring declaim
the branch of yew deplanes

every malice has its window
every kraken has its wake
every tipster plays the scoundrel
every dullard takes his cake

is it a matter of redress
that makes me so digress?
does a blunder torn asunder send
me thundering toward a sauna?

gag the piano and bait the snare
love is cruel and life unfair

Lyle Neff

SLEEPING ON THE WEIRD SIDE

OK, shift work's the assassin of sleep & health & marriages;
Fine, you never saw so many damp sunrises, god knows
You never want to again; I know, the last bus from downtown
Is crammed with wolves, casualties & hideous odours;

But don't you feel that predatory halo yourself, the vigour
Of difference? Consider an owl tracking thru the vulnerable
Night of a billion sleeping mice: you can be like that & kill!
Or maybe just decide not to. You can be a worker, *citoyen*,

& suffer a noontime dream that the sun is burning you, & come
into this world of toothbrushes, coffee stains, the landlord
at the door. OK, the fervour of life lived opposed to humanity
Is the unhealthiest drug; Fine, insomnia contains glamour; I know

That getting the work done costs & costs you, is jammed full
Of sloth & carrion wannabes & working bad hours—& years

Alfred G. Bailey

ELM

Look well upon the elm whose wittol root
roams like a hungry rat the eternal damp
and sorrowful ground, its gimlet face a clamp
upon a purpose as it tools for loot.
The faceless mold transmutes a slavering brute
to hang in all the wordless aisles of air
as green hosannas, tuned to trumpet fare
of sun-bedizened light, from claw to flute.
What wry design impels the furtive dark
to lift up day to wear its gothic pride?
Tree-eyed, the inchoate energies embark
upon a glory they themselves have died
to fashion, heedless of the slurring sound
of the blind and pointed faces underground.

Wayne Clifford

from *On Abducting the 'Cello*

3. In which we are asked to assume a value for vivisection

A rat hooked on the shock of pleasure starves.
The lab technician cleans the cage, zeroes
the counter, enters in the log heroes
by number, weight, and freedom that the wharves
will never hear of, pink-eyed troubadours
that improvised fate right on their brains. He shows
the kill to someone with a scalpel, mows
the skull fur off another batch. Remorse
can play no part in it. An unthot urge
is any cage the song itself declares
hunger's voice. Once feel the rubber glove
grasping the nape, the needle, then the surge
releasing perfect mercy, and the hairs
will stand stubbled in the skin for love.

Matt Rader

ELECTRIC CHAIR BY ANDY WARHOL

Ladies and gentlemen, prepare to be shocked
and amazed. This sturdy piece of oaken furniture,
fashioned with the love and grace of a master
carpenter—a real character—is expertly wired
with the very latest in solid state circuitry.
Complete with electrodes for the head and feet,
adjustable backrest, drip pan, Plexiglas seat,
and primed and painted with a high-gloss epoxy
developed for space, it is a state-of-the-art system
for all your electrocution needs. Plug-in
components, and a dose of pentobarbital sodium
no more than one half hour prior to execution,
makes no-hassle handling for any Jack Ketch
stuck awaiting the word to work the switch—

Joe Denham

THE SLEEPER IN THE VALLEY

On a lakeshore lined with alder, maple, fir
where the leaves, having let go, speckle the earth
auburn, crimson, vermeil, the water's stir
turning low autumn light like wheels of mirth,
a young man, slackened, leans back, the soft leather
of his car's front seat cradling him in sleep:
head aslant against the window, hands together,
fingers intertwined, prayerful in his lap.

He is napping, a slight grin on his face,
having fallen asleep to unburdened thoughts
of the coming winter, his life's pace
slowed to this stillness, the knot
in his stomach unspooled like the duct tape
sealing hose-ends to tailpipe and window.

Barbara Nickel

FOR PETER, MY COUSIN

The night you died I heard your cello shift—
a scraping in its corner of the barn.
Alfalfa pillowed it. White breath of pigs
was wreathed around the scroll; the cattle mourned.
For years its neck had rested by your ear.
Your bow across its strings and belly filled
the burlap sacks with apples, dusky tarns
of sound. You listened to that voice until
your marriage. Then she didn't let you play.
Her own voice, hoarse from children, saw you lean
in longing to the shovel, hurl the hay.
She felt your fingers press the strings in dream.
Your heart collapsed too soon—you died asleep.
Beside you she heard wood and horsehair weep.

David Manicom

AUTUMN EVENING SEES THROUGH
THE BLINDNESS OF PRAYER

Attached to parched darkness by a throat
The iron stove at night is like a brain.
I seem to sit willingly in *this* quiet.
Logs shift in the muttering stove, flame
Returns from where it has been folded
Down: a sudden animal of air, heart
Of the room. Somewhere limbs tilt, snag, hold—
A meteor scrapes the lake-thinned sky. I start,
Into sleep? Leg slips, swallowed oxygen flees
Into smoke where charred and jewelled lovers
Tense. Tied by cord to what I cannot see
I list upward waiting for the stirring lover
—shadowed by my stare's direction—to move me,
Start the superb stutter of need, flue's roar.

Wilfred Watson

TARQUIN

Not so, not so, she cries—but now he's lit
at death's white taper, and from its waxy
tongue takes flame her ravelled dress torn flax
to crumple in his flaring hands and light
flame firefling up to the burning roof hit
caught. Now she the burning house forsakes
but at her door with his rash hands he rakes
hot coals to fire the last beams sills of it.
And is become all loves incendiaries
who the dour cold traitorous house have sacked,
consideration, honour, marriage;
cold flesh is like a harlot, and complies
and her aching vein is filled with outrage
till he too sickens at his empty act.

John Reibetanz

RHODA

No one plants fireweed. The seeds must be hovering there
Like snow ignored indoors, ticking on
Through the first hiss of the match—or one with the ozone
Fuming from the struck tree after lightning; there,
Afloat on air the bushes' screams jar
When flames catch and strangle, white seed-puffs coast
Over the sea-roar of the dying forest,
And land like spacemen on a dry, charred shore.
It springs up from the dead places: pits
Black as the empty sockets of the moon
Bloom in tropic fury, and from their passion
Bees will distill the fire of the sun.
And the moon, white old magician, reaches in
And pulls red flowers from my emptiness.

Robyn Sarah

ON CLOSING THE APARTMENT OF MY
GRANDPARENTS OF BLESSED MEMORY

And then I stood for the last time in that room.
The key was in my hand. I held my ground,
and listened to the quiet that was like a sound,
and saw how the long sun of winter afternoon
fell slantwise on the floorboards, making bloom
the grain in the blond wood. (All that they owned
was once contained here.) At the window moaned
a splinter of wind. I would be going soon.

I would be going soon; but first I stood,
hearing the years turn in that emptied place
whose fullness echoed. Whose familiar smell,
of a tranquil life, lived simply, clung like a mood
or a long-loved melody there. A lingering grace.
Then I locked up, and rang the janitor's bell.

Crispin Elsted

SONNET WITH GRAMMAR LOOKING OVER THE WEALD OF KENT FROM BOUGHTON CHURCH

You can increase the distance sheep by weed
by looking first at the wall at the edge of a grave
and over it to the first copse where deer
engage grass and from there the windbreak of spoken trees
announces the mile in green curds
beyond which and over a stocked pond it hides
farms tuck and an utter smoke makes work
draw the fields around it with a jerk
before on a hedgerow the looking slides
a plain reach indistinguishing birds
in haze-deckle phrasing three oasts and the bees
succumb words behind my arm and mere
nouns are naming verbs nudge particles place and wave
and grammar is distance in memory of Charles John Meade.

D.C. Scott

WATKWENIES

Vengeance was once her nation's lore and law:
When the tired sentry stooped above the rill,
Her long knife flashed, and hissed, and drank its fill;
Dimly below her dripping wrist she saw,
One wild hand, pale as death and weak as straw,
Clutch at the ripple in the pool; while shrill
Sprang through the dreaming hamlet on the hill,
The war-cry of the triumphant Iroquois.

Now clothed with many an ancient flap and fold,
And wrinkled like an apple kept till May,
She weighs the interest-money in her palm,
And, when the Agent calls her valiant name,
Hears, like the war-whoops of her perished day,
The lads playing snow-snake in the stinging cold.

David Hickey

PRESERVATION

These boys will never outgrow their jean jackets,
this photograph, the cliffs and the tattered maps

the wind wears into them. They will not lose
their way among the shoreline's rocky bruises,

or forget where the best spots are to hide
from the heat of an afternoon sun. It's the tide,

this boy, and the way he points at a wave
that will preserve them, the hand and how

it staves their leaving: they're looking down,
perhaps at some broken piece of driftwood

crowned with rotting seaweed, some bundle swept
from the camera's flash. None of them expect

to be preserved this carefully, their hands
in their pockets, or pulling up strands of grass.

Peter Dale Scott

from "SPACE SONNETS"

PLANH

So I have no more hair in back,
only a joke of a tonsure, that's o.k.
as long as I don't have to see it.

But this! to have nose-hairs in my ears,
a beard that is working up my nose,
to be *the arhat of the shaggy eyebrows*

Nature, butt off! if I ever thought
of you as parent, to be trusted,
forget about it. You should have quit

when you covered up my chicken-breast
with unasked for curls. Now I want
the earmarks neither of a savage man

nor of a holy one   to be free
of all signs   even that word *me*

Evie Christie

OLD MEN SITTING IN DIZENGOFF
SQUARE AT NIGHT

Or Christie Pits in the blackout, don't worry
about weather patterns, the price of gasoline
or leaks that sing their poverty
from ceiling tiles and faucets. They don't
think about lumps in the breast that spread
and degraded the women who wrapped
their sandwiches for work or war and swollen
with babies broke ceramic mugs not so far
from their dinner seats. They eat radishes
and apples, drink homemade wine
and remind me that it's absurd to dream about
the shallow grave we placed the robin in that summer,
beneath leaves and damp grass until rain exposed us
in the tiny bones and soft matted feathers.

Raymond Souster

YOUNG GIRLS

With night full of spring and stars we stand
here in this dark doorway and watch the young
girls pass, two, three together, hand in hand.
They are like flowers whose fragrance hasn't sprung
or awakened, whose bodies now dimly feel
the flooding, upward welling of the trees;
whose senses, caressed by the wind's soft fingers, reel
with a mild delirium that makes them ill at ease.

They lie awake at night, unable to sleep,
then walk the streets, kindled by strange desires;
they steal lightning glances at us, unable to keep
control upon those subterranean fires.
We whistle after them, then laugh, for they
stiffen, not knowing what to do or say.

Elizabeth Bachinsky

HOW TO BAG YOUR SMALL TOWN GIRL

Those small-town girls they like to marry
early you know. Can't wait to settle down, have
a kid or two. What they wouldn't give
for a solid man, one that's ready
to rein it in—that rampant prick—and stick
close to home, a good father, provider
and lover, a tall drink of water
who's cool when the pick-up's bust, stick-
shift stuck in second gear or the condom's broke
again. But there's no such thing as too much man
to handle, hon. Those girls, they like men rough
around the edges, tough boys who'll never balk
at next month's rent and heart enough to love
a woman right, again and again and again.

Suzanne Buffam

MEANWHILE

But could not keep so let seep in the wind.
So rolled the windows down and let it roar.
So felt the fingerbones inside me find
the fingered thing inside this foreign core.

So thickened by the inches, minutes, and the miles,
it hurled us into onwards and so through
the wet blue rolling landscape meanwhile's
made of where we're quickened and most true.

So made of us a place we can return to
when we're far. We are. We're far
from where we've been so far and who. It's you—

It's you to whom I'm speaking now so far
from you with whom I'll lie down when we're through.
So loosed the breathing we inside we are.

Leonard Cohen

YOU HAVE NO FORM

You have no form, you move among, yet do
not move, the relics of exhausted thought
of which you are not made, but which give world to
you, who are of nothing made, nothing wrought.
There you long for one who is not me, O
queen of no subject, newer than the morning,
more antique than first seed dropped below
the wash where you are called and Adam born.
And here, not your essence, not your absence
weds the emptiness which is never me,
though these motions and these formless events
are preparation for humanity,
and I get up to love and eat and kill
not by my own, but by our married will.

Archibald Lampman

WINTER EVENING

To-night the very horses springing by
Toss gold from whitened nostrils. In a dream
The streets that narrow to the westward gleam
Like rows of golden palaces; and high
From all the crowded chimneys tower and die
A thousand aureoles. Down in the west
The brimming plains beneath the sunset rest,
One burning sea of gold. Soon, soon shall fly
The glorious vision, and the hours shall feel
A mightier master; soon from height to height,
With silence and the sharp unpitying stars,
Stern creeping frosts, and winds that touch like steel,
Out of the depth beyond the eastern bars,
Glittering and still shall come the awful night.

George Ellenbogen

THE SKATERS

Extending hands, we shape the ice in games
by poles of light that sluice upon the pond.
Through pines the moon had shown; now slipped beyond
where skaters cannot see or skate their names.
Now only blackness, such a blackness now
as hides all sight of trees, stiff reeds that sprout
by ice we marked gliding deft figures out
from side to side, and in a truce (although
we scarcely see beneath our knees) blow
a hot skater's breath that leaves no trace
as we slice wider rings and wider race
leaning from the edge where dark shapes grow,
tilting parallel, holding tight,
our arms a skipping rope for leaps of night.

Ken Babstock

FIRST LESSON IN UNPOPULAR MECHANICS

As a boy, it was a scale-model Messerschmitt
pitched at the wall in a boy-scale rage—
Now? These grown-up middletones, wafflings, shit
flung deliberately wide of the fan. I remember the age
I began to ease off—thirteen, fourteen—
when busting one's stick meant a five-minute major,
and there, in the sin bin, thinking, *what did I mean
by two-handing the crossbar?* Couldn't gauge or
properly reckon what point I had made (hoped
I had made) so kept my caged gaze on the raftered clock:
that massive, red-rashed, free-floating block
where the seconds of my sentence, my stasis, loped
towards zero, zero, and zero in slow-mo.
The thing opposed, absolutely, my re-entering play; its rules,
   its flow.

Walid Bitar

TARZAN

In wrestling and poetry, everything is staged.
Contestants rehearse their pins and holds.
For artifice to work, it must be faked;
those with the least sincerity soar.

One can spin a tale of self-sacrifice
best if his temper finds heroes vain.
Feeling every word one utters is a swelling
that warps a surface, and bruises the fun.

Hard to be certain; it often happens
we can't decide if we mean what we say,
a state never listed with the deadly sins,
this taking of pleasure in our deep disarray.

Friends, it bores me to know where I stand;
a meditating Tarzan needs quicksand.

Peter Norman

BOLSHEVIK TENNIS!

Haul down the nets. Erase the painted lines
That separate the people from the court.
Blot out every logo: thwart the designs
Of those who would make profit of the sport.

Let service serve; let ranking be repealed.
Cast off your bourgeois white; dress up in red.
Put down the racket you were taught to wield
And raise the racket of revolt instead.

Dethrone the umpire and his random will—
His proclamations have been foul indeed!
Let each man play according to his skill;
Let each man score according to his need.

And some day yet, we shall be free of score:
Love will serve love—game, set and evermore.

Milton Acorn

THE COMPLETION OF THE FIDDLE (N.M.)

The fiddle's incomplete without the dance;
My darling. Let's hook fingers to complete
By motion to the calls, the sweet riddle
Of the tune now wriggling in the soft wind
On top of which the bright moon goes riding;
For if no happy bottoms prance and spin
Upon the planks and polish what's it all worth—
That round of steamed, shaped, rehardened wood
Varnished as it's put about a hollow
From which a tune may radiate its mirth
By the merry rub of gut against gut?
The candles flicker and the stars twinkle
All to be parts of the completed fiddle!

Robert Finch

THE PRUNUS

The fountain's iron lady, freshly stained
Black, wrings her black hair before a clump
Of fresh bamboo, jet locks not a whit damp
Yet always wrung beyond the water's feigned

Fresh wish to mesh those tresses in glass braids
Which twisting skyward from the bowl's black brow
Dash thwarted toward the pool of shades below
To split along the yucca's shadowed blades.

Black baffles white until the purple prunus,
Gashed by the sun, splashing the water ruddy,
Persuades the irony of the iron lady
To smiling fire, the fountain's light to noon, as

From raven strand is wrung the rosy dew
Of wine, down blushing yucca, pink bamboo.

P.K. Page

WATER AND MARBLE

And shall I tell him that the thought of him
turns me to water
and when his name is spoken pale still sky
trembles and breaks and moves like blowing water
that winter thaws its frozen drifts in water
all matter blurs, unsteady, seen through water
and I, in him, dislimn, water in water?

As true: the thought of him
has made me marble
and when his name is spoken blowing sky
settles and freezes in a dome of marble
and winter seals its floury drifts in marble
all matter double-locks as dense as marble
and I, in other's eyes, am cut from marble.

Richard Sanger

ONCE OF THE GANG

My love, though I live in the suburbs now,
Remember the nights, the summer nights downtown,
The nights we'd ride our bikes through rapturous streets,
The cafe by the canal where we'd meet
Whoever it was—it was always urgent—
Discuss the answer to life (one word, French)
While the moon above, no less earnest,
Did its best in our existential universe.
Yes, and then the night the outsider came
To ask his question and whisk me away . . .
All that history sunk like pipes beneath the pool
I've ended up beside—the turquoise pool,
The lime green grass, the lilac boughs.
I told you: I live in the suburbs now.

Adam Sol

SONNET WITH THE MORNING PAPER

We've got grackles stealing morning from the sun,
reluctant, enmeshed in telephone wire.
A raucous tribe, red squirrels conspire
to chatter the neighbourhood from their homes.
Dawn-sensitive streetlights flicker off,
spooking sparrows. Red maple crowded with finches,
starlings, and a crow, Dumpsters and mesh fences.
The bright air—clouds raspy, green, and lost.
A neighbour on his porch whistles "Misty"
over a bossy, grumbling garbage truck.
Hotshot paperboy in his rolling bag of rust
plants a story of the world into our heads:
it is brief, big, and black. Somewhere fifty
students have joined the bloated ranks of the dead.

Gerry Gilbert

BANNOCK

safe at home
no-one
will ever know

open the door one morning
where in the world
did the earth go

robin
magpie
redwing blackbird

ate it
cold
flew away

laid it someplace new
& old

Phyllis Webb

POETICS AGAINST THE ANGEL OF DEATH

I am sorry to speak of death again
(some say I'll have a long life)
but last night Wordsworth's 'Prelude'
suddenly made sense—I mean the measure,
the elevated tone, the attitude
of private Man speaking to public men.
Last night I thought I would not wake again
but now with this June morning I run ragged to elude
The Great Iambic Pentameter
who is the Hound of Heaven in our stress
because I want to die
writing Haiku
or, better,
long lines, clean and syllabic as knotted bamboo. Yes!

George Whipple

POETRY

Who monograms each snowflake with his mark?

Whose voice is howling echoes in the eave?

The long, cold, lonely nights of winter warm
consumers with canned visions on TV
while poets, brooding in damp basements, dark,
whittle air into the shape of sound—pure form.

Self-made martyrs in a private universe,
they hammer shadow-nails in shadow-wood;
carpenters, all thumbs, the sorrow in their blood
to raise themselves, thorn-crowned, self-sacrificed,
upon a paper cross, no longer self-despised,
relieving hairshirt conscience with a verse;
hanging from their poems, self-redeemed, aloof,
as if words outlast the snowdrifts on the roof.

Robert Allen

SONNET OF NOTHING

And given nothing, the order ramifies. It includes
autumn, a damning and thinning, and hiding
in the cruel winter months. And given nothing,

my job, fifty hours a week, becomes what I think
is a governing love for all the people I work with.
The people I teach, they are so fragile and trusting,

that education will lift them out of everything,
when it will not even lift them out of the north wind.
They and I are teetering on the brink, but bring

a grace and creativity, and maybe most important
a denial of the end of everything. The metred instants
in sweeping storms, the moments when you trust

your life means something: that is when the moon
comes around in its swing, to shine on our ruin.

John Smith

THERE IS ONE

There is one metaphor for everything. If it is money,
then poetry is redundant. If not—ah, if not, then
is it that single nonsense syllable sung by the indefatigable
oarsman setting his back against the tide of things,

groaning out the strokes of his trade, but hearing
in each groan a new thwack of the sea ring
like an unstoppable tonic chord reached at the last
expiring bar in the last sonata of a long career

as the boat turns to flotsam? Yes, it is that.
There is one metaphor that serves for everything in turn,
and it is like enough to all metaphors at once that it hardly
        differs from

the things themselves that hardly differ from the effort to
        achieve them.
Bend, address the moment—this is an old see-saw—drop
—get it right—heave, breathe, groan, hear, swing up, again,
        again.

NOTES ON THE POEMS

M. Travis Lane, "The Talisman": Like the stone Lane writes of, and like many of the small lyrics by Dickinson it echoes, this trim little sonnet seems almost "significant of nothing." But things get very interesting after the turn, with the paradoxical notion of a "nothing" failing the speaker and the transformation, through metaphor, of the safe, comprehensible talisman into a beating heart. Lane does the miraculous here: she draws blood from a stone.

David W. McFadden, "Country Hotel in the Niagara Peninsula": This free-verse sonnet, the last line of which echoes and complicates Rilke's "You must change your life," puts the vault back into volta. In a note on the poem, McFadden helpfully describes it as a "split-level poem, with what appears at first to be no apparent connection between the two stanzas." Clearly, appearances can apparently appear to be deceptive.

Don Coles, "Sampling from a Dialogue": Doesn't look much like a sonnet, does it? Don't be fooled. It starts off quite orthodox, the first three lines an approximation of pentameter. Then they start getting shaggier, stretching out, but the rhyme scheme stays intact until line twelve, after which, with the introduction of the wife's voice, the whole structure falls apart, as does the husband's idle fantasy. But look closely: structurally, those last eight lines function as two lines – the concluding couplet – and they do rhyme; "rhyme" is even one of the rhyming words! Everything in this poem is so casual and yet so artfully contrived. It is, really, a sonnet about how to write sonnets when they're silly and old-fashioned (like the husband's "obviously inflated" daydream analogy, the sonnet, like Roland, a medieval

European relic), overused ("we have been through / this forty thousand times") and you're sick of hearing them ("I need to hear something different"). Look at the details: the brilliant line break "let's have a new / line," just as the lines of the poem start to transgress the bounds of prosodic decorum; the shopworn poetics of "consoling pose[s]" that are "all used up"; the speaker's conscious awareness that the wife's matter-of-fact answer is "breaking the rhyme"; the epiphanic revelation that the couple was unconsciously "making" a new kind of poetic "clarity." The argument here is not just between man and wife, but on a metaphorical level between poet and form; Coles' particular resolution is a shining example of how to innovate without throwing out the baby of poetic heritage with the bathwater of versification's stagnation.

Don McKay, "Stress, Shear, and Strain Theories of Failure": This is an unusual feature in the oeuvre of Don McKay, who normally eschews anything resembling set forms. This one, from his most recent collection, makes me hope there's more in this vein to come. The demands of the rhyme scheme, however loosely he tries to meet them, seem to rein in the sometimes erratic flight of his improvisatory meditations. Terrific tension created by inserting the dramatic movements of tectonic plates into the cozy confines of a sonnet. Really, compared with your average igneous rock, the sonnet's a new kid on the block.

Michael Parr, "Palimpsest": Parr's a very recent discovery for me. I sought out his 1965 book *The Green Fig Tree* in the library on a tip from Wayne Clifford, who wasn't even sure if he remembered Parr's name aright. Easy to see how an English expat writing poems like this in the sixties might slip into obscurity. I don't think I've ever encountered a sonneteer as consistently bent on making things harder for himself. Just look at the consonantal para-rhymes he uses, with only slight vowel variations. In some of his poems, the strain of such troubadourish constraints cripples the poem, but the experiment proves worthwhile in one like this. There's something Welsh about this kind of formal straitjacketing, and one can certainly hear echoes of Dylan Thomas in lines like "whose lad of words leaps in the dying man." Whatever happened to Michael Parr? Where is he now?

Margaret Avison, "Snow": What a fantastically assertive opening. And it's all gorgeously original image and metaphor thereafter, coined in aural splendor and served with syntactic dash and verve. Avison didn't write many sonnets, but this one, along with her "Tennis" and "Butterfly Bones: Sonnet Against Sonnets," are among the best published in the last century, for my money.

Stuart Ross, "The Children of Mary Crawl Back at Night": Even Ross's best poems seem to have been tossed off in ten minutes flat, scribbled on diner napkins. The first eleven lines, rapid-fire and heavily enjambed, of this loose sonnet enact the manic mood of the mother coping with small children, literally at loose ends, but then Ross deftly strings lines twelve through fourteen out to a more orthodox five stress beat, and introduces end-stops, miming exhaustion, culminating in the seemingly out-of-nowhere but deeply moving rhyming conclusion. A very sneaky sonnet.

Eric Ormsby, "Childhood Pieties": Ormsby grew up in the southern U.S. – and look what it did to him! What a creepy, daring way to end this modified Italian number, twisting it from social satire to personal Freudian nightmare.

Christopher Wiseman, "Departure Gate": Wiseman's voice is so straightforward in the opening lines of this sonnet that banality alarms start ringing. Oh god, the poet talking to his son about writing

– or worse, not writing – a sonnet; how precious! But then, the surprise of what the speaker sees seems to disarm him, as the abab scheme of the first quatrain clumps into an awkward ccdd, or consonantally cccc; the prosodic equivalent of the poet getting choked up. But he does "recover" in the sestet, and fulfills his promise to write the requested sonnet. The unusual device of a closing apostrophe is justified by what comes before, which makes its restrained emotion all the more powerful.

George Johnston, "Cathleen Sweeping": Johnston is one of our trickiest formal poets. He builds this sonnet into mirrors; notice how both halves of the octave (especially with both first and eighth lines ending with the same word) and the sestet reflect each other and how this perfectly contains the speaker's own reflection on how the seemingly purposeless and futile work (again, the contrast of small child and infinite sky, with the art of sweeping in between) of his young daughter is like his own "small and busy" thoughts. The sonneteer must work by design, he must "think it through," but must also accommodate child-like "delight."

Amanda Jernigan, "Lullaby": Jernigan has yet to publish her first book, but this mythologically-inflected Petrarchan variant augurs well. Not only the subject matter, but the diction of this poem and the apparent effortlessness of its stops and enjambments, imbue it with a timeless feeling. If there is a "trick of making," then Jernigan has clearly learned it from the masters.

Diana Brebner, "What Is Homeless in Me, and Sightless": Brebner breaks the quatrains into couplets, but this is a Shakespearean sonnet. At her best, Brebner can wring an improbable amount of emotion out of very modest technique. The rhymes in this poem are textbook faux pas: nondescript pronouns and adverbs; abstract nouns – "darkness" not once, but twice, including the last line! – and adjectives; the clangingly obvious "sight" and "fight." There are a number of abstractions embedded within the lines, too, in blatant contradiction of Pound's dictum to go in fear of the critters if you want to be a proper modern poet. And yet, the poem sustains and transcends its apparent shortcomings, somehow. In part, it's the tension between the artlessness of the phrasing and the cunning structure of the thing; if read aloud, you hardly hear the rhymes. But it's clinched by the apostrophe to the beloved in line twelve. The concluding couplet accounts convincingly for why everything above is so vague – for why it has to be.

David Solway, "I'm writing this because I'm desperate.": David Solway is known to be one of the most outspoken and acerbic critics of the plainspoken and prosy in Canadian poetry. Here he shows that his advocacy of form cannot be properly understood as a "formalist" clarion call for a return to archaic "poetic" diction. This Shakespearean sonnet, drawn from a sequence of love sonnets published in the very sonnet-unfriendly 1980s, is a lovely example of how to fit colloquial speech to elegant metrical structures. I love the directness of that first line, and the intimacy of what follows. And what an *osé* move, rhyming the beloved's name with "barren"!

Sharon McCartney, "Impending Death of the Cat": A deftly turned Shakespearean sonnet, the surprising final line casting all previous lines in a new light. The unexpected metaphor of cat-as-bridge thus becomes not merely a novel, but a necessary image. The sonnet – old, yet persistently vital, hanging on to life despite the vicious vicissitudes of time – seems a particularly apt choice of form for this elegiac love poem.

Mike Barnes, "First Stab": Atypically, this sonnet is written in loose tetrameter couplets. This formal decision helps create an ironic playfulness, a singsongy rhythm, that works in tension with the darkness of the subject matter. The combination is quite unsettling.

J.D. Black, "Antiheroic Couplets": Another sonnet in couplets, this one a dramatic monologue. Black uses enjambment skillfully to make this tight structure sound very conversationally natural. The slant rhyme at the end of the last line – stretched to an alexandrine by the insertion of the parenthetical "staring," chiming internally with "scared" – is a particularly deft touch. Black's own story is quite interesting. He came to poetry relatively late in life, publishing his first book at 55 after working a variety of jobs. Clearly, he hasn't worried too much about building a literary career *comme il faut*.

Goran Simić, "I Was a Fool": Simić lived through the siege of Sarajevo and much of his most powerful writing in verse and prose is concerned with that bloody episode in European history. Simić is now resident in Toronto and this Shakespearean sonnet is one of the first poems he has written in English. This poem is relentless in both its structure (note that all of the first twelve lines rhyme, consonantally) and in the self-examination of the speaker/poet who consumes death and destruction for the purposes of art.

Ralph Gustafson, ""S.S.R. Lost at Sea." –*The Times*": A hard thing to pull off, the public memorial, and not a terribly fashionable thing to write occasional verse of any sort in the age of lyricism and irony, but Gustafson, a poet much underrated in recent decades, does a more than creditable job with this Shakespearean/Petrarchan hybrid. I particularly like how he jams up syntax, disrupting flow in an emotionally affecting manner.

E.J. Pratt, "The Ground Swell": Known more for his long narrative poems, Pratt shows he's a dab hand at shorter forms with this virtuoso single-sentence sonnet which pits the finite human against the eternal primeval force of the sea. Sound familiar?

Anita Lahey, "In Which Your Uncle Recalls the Last Time He Traversed the Treacherous Tittle on the Way to Scaterie": Lahey does a brilliant job of wedding the vernacular muscle of Cape Breton speech to the formal intricacies of the Italian sonnet. "Tittle" is a dialect term for a narrow and treacherous strait.

Kenneth Leslie, from "By Stubborn Stars": Canadians have a terrible habit of forgetting some of their best poets whilst canonizing mediocrities. Leslie is one such forgotten poet, though there seems to be a modest renascence of interest in his work. The 28-sonnet sequence from which this poem is taken, depicting a tumultuous love triangle, is one of the most moving and perfectly made long poems in Canadian literary history. It is, alas, out of print. Leslie's handling of the pentameter is supplely flexible – only six of fourteen lines have ten syllables, and I love the subtle but aurally discernible effect of the eleventh line swelling to thirteen syllables. The diction is simple, direct and clear, the content traditional: a poem of love expressed obliquely through a single controlling metaphorical conceit. What sets it apart is the perfect fitness of its parts. Start with the repetitions: the teeming sheen of "silver"; the triple affirmation of "life"; the added weight of "heavy"; the insistent "stress of rowing"; the lullaby of world, world, world; the synchronicity of cries and strokes on shore and at sea. The end-rhymes contribute to this piled-on pairing effect – note, especially, the lovely and unlikely match of a humbly concrete "dory" with triumphant abstract "glory," mirrored by the complementary pairing of "seine" and "pain," setting up the poem's metaphorical twin planes. Alliterative patterns also do heavy lifting, all those sibilants in the first lines miming the slippery vigour of fish that "throbbed thick," that double-stress with no space emphasizing the heaving plenty of the catch; the hard k-sounds so evocative of cold and cuts; the relentless pain of labour captured by "hands," "hurt," "hauling," "heavy," "heavy"; the slow spoken progress of "life," "low" and "lips," picked up again by "length," "landing" and "low" once more; the trough and crest of waves in "pain," "pulled," "plunged," "pulse," "puts," the quickened approach of "stroke," "stroke," "steadily," echoed in the last line by "straight," anchoring the journey's end, "threshold," "threw" and "through," more spaced out this time, but bringing us full-circle to the erotic thrum of the poem's first line. This is a stanza jammed to the gunwales with energetic tensions of sound and sense.

Brenda Tate, "The Last Mate": Tate here shows a masterful handling of the six-stress alexandrine, not only using end-rhyme effortlessly, but just look at how studded her lines are with internal rhyme, assonance and alliteration. Terrific turns of phrase too, like "star-spackle spit," "juddered and swung and fell" and "arrowed the air on a sprit." A poet who definitely deserves a wider audience.

Charles Bruce, "Early Morning Landing": Like Kenneth Leslie, Bruce is another outstanding Nova Scotian poet who has suffered unjust posthumous neglect, though this should be redressed in part by the forthcoming publication of a new selection of his verse and prose. Though he was from Nova Scotia, Bruce did most of his writing about the province in Toronto, where he was a highly respected journalist. The sad truth of Maritime life is that many of the region's sons and daughters, although fiercely rooted in their communities, must leave them to make a decent living. But we probably wouldn't have Bruce's poetry as it exists without this. This hybrid English/Italian sonnet touchingly reflects the experience of Bruce's voluntary exile and homesickness, "the faint recurring spark / Of a known beacon."

Steven Price, "Rope:": The problem with a lot of list poems is that they go on and on and don't come to any real point, but Price uses the sonnet to give shape to a metaphorical inventory, the poem uncoiling like a spool of rope and suddenly snapping to a stop with the couplet. A virtuoso adaptation of the sonnet form to litany, and vice-versa.

Carmine Starnino, "Rope Husbandry": Starnino mines the jargon of knots to its full metaphorical potential, rejuvenating the sad old cliché about "tying the knot." And notice how he cinches his blank sonnet tight with rhyme in the last four lines – though I would argue that a more intricate knotwork of thought and sound-rhyme runs through the poem as a whole, particularly on the end-words of lines – to give formal shape to the nasty bit of wit at the end.

John Barton, "Saint Joseph's Hospital, 1937": This poem is taken from Barton's book *West of Darkness: Emily Carr, A Self-Portrait*. Carr's a favourite topic for Canadian poets in search of a Canadian Theme, but rarely treated with the kind of formal discipline displayed by Barton here – a bit of a surprise to those who know him more for his long-lined couplets. A very orthodox Petrarchan sonnet, in terms of rhyme scheme and metre, but kept loose by deft enjambments and vivified by dense patterns of internal rhyme, assonance and alliteration.

Steven Heighton, "Missing Fact": Steven Heighton, since his 1994 collection, *The Ecstasy of Skeptics*, has been at the vanguard of a generation of Canadian poets renovating traditional forms into contemporary relevance. "Missing Fact" is a crafty piece of work, starting out as a verse essay on one of the English language's oldest sonnets and shifting into the sonnet's traditional preoccupation: romantic love and its failing. *Plus ça change, plus c'est la même chose*. And lovely how

Heighton uses slant rhymes consistently, cleverly echoing the poem's subject in its structure.

Shane Neilson, "Rural Gothic": Neilson writes of love's verso in this moving portrait of the difficulty of loving difficult people in difficult situations. Notice how the rhymes are irregular in the octave, only "frost" and "lost" standing out, the scheme as "weather-beaten" as the crops, but then, as the attempt at love is made, the rhymes galvanize, so that in the almost identical rhyme of the couplet, the link between violence and love is made undeniable.

Fred Cogswell, "Valley-Folk": With his anaphoric repetition of "narrow" – echoing Elizabeth Bishop's line about "narrow prov-inces/of fish and bread and tea" – in the octave, Cogswell evokes biblical psalms and constricts the formal possibilities available to him. Then, in the sestet, the introduction of the river that "mocks the patterned fields that we enclose" widens the poem as well. And in case you think he's cheating a bit, "Sundays" is a perfect rhyme with "Grundies" in most parts of the Maritimes.

Alden Nowlan, "St. John River": One of the great fallacies in critical talk about Nowlan is that when he made the transition from rhyme and metre to a more conversational free-verse approach he truly came into his own. This irregularly-rhymed sonnet shows just how subtle and supple Nowlan could be within the constraints of traditional forms. This is a great poem in part because it eschews the sentimental-ity of earlier pastoral poems about the region and damns the lies of tourist brochures while still affirming the river's beauty.

Geoffrey Cook, "The next tide wipes away the muddy shoal": This is a pretty faithful translation of Rilke's sonnet, but Cook, a Nova

Scotian by birth, adapts Rilke's French dykelands into the Acadian dykelands of his home province by using a characteristic east-coast expression in the last line. Voilà!

Charles G.D. Roberts, "The Potato Harvest": Ah, the quiescent sublimity of it all! This sonnet is like an impressionist painting. Roberts doesn't have much to say, but the description's lovely, is it not?

W.W. Campbell, "At Even": A deliciously wicked satire of the pastoral conventions and overblown bathos of the poetry of Campbell's day. Campbell had a greater affinity for the political themes of Archibald Lampman and D.C. Scott than for the prettiness of Roberts and Bliss Carman.

David O'Meara, "Postcard from Camus": A witty incorporation of casual colloquialism and formal excellence that undercuts the seriousness of Camus' existentialism. The thought of Camus uttering a platitude like "Wish you were here" – particularly after he's made "here" sound so bloody miserable – is hilarious.

George Elliott Clarke, "Negation": The strong-stress rhythm, wordplay, alliteration and macaronic diction of this irregularly rhymed sonnet is classic Clarke, bombastic and unabashed. Like Derek Walcott and other politically engaged black poets, Clarke understands that it's better, and more politically effective, to re-colonize the language and forms of Europe than to reject them entirely in favour of "deconstructed" post-colonial texts.

Daryl Hine, "1er *Palais Royal*": Hine is one of the last century's most accomplished technicians, and this sonnet is pure showoffy fun, as he uses only two rhymes and a clutch of clever word and sound combinations. Notice how he elides "slang which" to rhyme with "language" and how "from age" if pronounced *en français*, rhymes perfectly with "*dommage*" – and means cheese. As he says, "Beware of the sound,/…/Sense can take care of itself." A credo for a sonneteer if ever there was one.

Nancy Holmes, "Can a Sonnet Be a Joke?": A wittily self-referential, raunchy Shakespearean sonnet, from a book called *The Adultery Poems*. If there's still any doubt about the possibility of writing sexually liberated feminist verse in "patriarchal" forms – though anyone who's read Edna St. Vincent Millay should know that's bunk – it doesn't seem to bother Holmes one bit.

Irving Layton, "Sagebrush Classic": Even if he said it himself many times too often, Irving Layton is arguably the greatest Canadian poet of all time. Though he wasn't prolific as a sonneteer, this nasty little Petrarchan gem showcases Layton at the top of his game. The allusions to Swift, Luther and Shakespeare are typical of Layton's literary ambition. He saw himself not so much as Canadian – he rarely missed a chance to voice his contempt of his home country – as a citizen of the literary world, an heir – and peer – of the great writers from a wide array of places and times. His preoccupations were far more world-historical than local, except insofar as he wished to shock Canadians out of what he saw to be their fundamental gentility. Although words like "faecal," "shit" and "fuckface" are more common in Canadian poems now than they were in Layton's early days, many of our leading idealists and sentimentalists could still stand to learn a thing or two from him about poetic diction.

E.A. Lacey, "We were the land's before the land was ours": As an openly gay man in the 1950s, Lacey had good cause to hate his country, which he spent as much time away from as he could. Bitingly ironic how he subverts the opening line of Frost's patriotic paean to

America. A shame no one got him to read it at the swearing in of John Diefenbaker . . .

Malcolm Lowry, "Delirium at Vera Cruz": Although better known as a novelist, Lowry thought of himself as a poet and left behind a substantial body of poetry, largely unpublished – even unfinished – at the time of his death, but much of it of very high quality. Many of those poems were composed in his shack in Dollarton, near North Vancouver. Like *Under the Volcano*, this sonnet is set in Mexico and its protagonist is a self-destructive alcoholic. I love how the unexpected ending ironizes all the self-drama that precedes it, putting a price tag on the character's pain.

Colin Carberry, "Abattoir": Interesting to compare this infernal dystopia to Charles G.D. Roberts' rural idyll [p. 46], because they're both built using the same basic procedure of evocative impressionistic description. But Carberry's deftly limned scene clearly has an unsettling impact on its painter, who can't – or won't – maintain the same degree of aloof detachment as Roberts' speaker.

Joe Rosenblatt & Catherine Owen, "Pounce": Something you don't see every day: this loose sonnet (not quite free – note the occasional slant rhymes) is a collaboration by two poets, part of a sequence of sonnets about dogs by Rosenblatt and Owen, with photographs by Karen Moe. In this particular poem, spoken in the voice of a *perro Cubano*, Rosenblatt does the octave and Owen the sestet. Both sonneteers seem to have a little mad dog in them.

Pino Coluccio, "The Time We Won the Cup in '82": Coluccio's loosely metred Italian sonnet (what else?) movingly reflects the immigrant experience of being in between places and the transient triumph of "little guys." And what a terrific simile he ends with!

Anne Wilkinson, "School of Hygiene": Wilkinson's rhythms here are strongly reminiscent of Dickinson, but it's hard to imagine Dickinson being so nasty!

A.J.M. Smith, "The Wisdom of Old Jelly Roll": Besides being a poet, Smith was also a prominent critic who, as a young man in 1928 (*plus ça change . . .*), called for less nationalistic sentimentality and more technique and awareness of tradition in Canadian poetry. This Shakespearean number carries a similar message and is both improvisatory and letter-perfect. Note how Smith extends the last line to a fourteener for emphasis.

Joshua Trotter, "The Teacher and the Peach": A terrific cascade of imagery and metaphor, given shape not only by the end-rhymes, but the internal patterns of soundplay. This sonnet really is bursting at the seams.

Molly Peacock, "The Lull": Like so many sonnets, this is a sort of *ars poetica*. Peacock says in very simple terms (just look at the exclusively monosyllabic third line and the abbreviated final line with its tripartite repetition of "flesh" to hammer the point home) that no matter how "disgusting" or ugly something is, the poet must look at it without flinching.

Stephen Brockwell, "The Fruitfly": Don't let the lack of end-rhyme fool you into thinking this free-verse sonnet is sloppily built. The thought articulated in this poem is every bit as intricate as the fruit fly's wing – if more nimble than the fly clapped into a punctuation mark. The metaphoric imagination Brockwell displays here reminds me of the pattern-perception of Hopkins in his journal prose. And in case you're wondering about his skill with more traditionally structured sonnets, you should seek out *Wild Clover Honey and the Bee-*

hive, a sequence of 28 sonnets on the sonnet – fourteen written by Brockwell, contra the form, and fourteen by Peter Norman, another contributor to this anthology, arguing for it. It's a brilliant performance of dialectical banjos.

George Amabile, "Poached Grilse": Another veiled *ars poetica*: if the poems don't come on their own, then go deep for them. Amabile's rhyme scheme is unusual; the octave is pretty straightforward Italian, but then the first line of the sestet rhymes with six and seven of the octave and "clean" rhymes assonantally with those lines, but consonantally with the lines that follow. And Amabile defies our expectations by using the same perfect rhyme for each of the last four lines, introducing a comic effect to complement the content of the closing two lines, which undercut the more meditatively serious tone that predominates in the rest of the poem – and along with it his rationalized justification for poaching (perhaps the speaker intends also to "poach" the grilse in wine . . .). Very cleverly built.

Tim Bowling, "Pacific Sockeye, Moving East": Bowling cheats a bit here with a throwaway two-stress opener, but the following thirteen lines are so good we should forgive him. The pace and rhythm of this unrhymed sonnet make a perfect match for the salmon's dynamic upriver struggle, and the metaphorical leaps Bowling makes are like the fish jumping up out of the water. I said unrhymed, but the sound effects are hardly muted and notice the gorgeous way the last word, "skin" picks up "sin" four lines earlier.

Eric Cole, "Right Whale": Cole is an elephant keeper by day, but this blank sonnet shows he knows his marine mammoths too. Terrific imagery here, that's no mere ornament; did you know, for instance, that girdles for women were once made from the baleen of right whales?

It's a fact. And what a magnificent visual and sonic metaphor to wallop the poem shut.

Mary Dalton, "Winter Coal": Part of what makes this seemingly rough-cut narrative sonnet work so well is Dalton's handling of the line. Listen to the sing-song rhythm of the octave, then look what happens after the turn. The sestet's lines pull in, the first three lines having eight syllables, the next two – at the point of dramatic climax – five each, and the last one eight again. And all but two words in the sestet are monosyllabic – a desperate, hard-bitten clinging-on effect.

Patrick Warner, "The Turn": A mesmerizing, snake-eating-its-tail sort of sonnet, eerily reminiscent of "The House that Jack Built." No rhyme scheme, as such, but held together in part by the chiming of "bell, tell, ill, hill, bell." Notice also how Warner seems to be commenting on his own procedures, making "the turn" in line four – an unusual place for it – and then hinging again after line eight, a more usual place.

George Murray, "Ditch": A poet will occasionally, when stuck for a sonic rhyme, substitute a "thought rhyme" or "concept rhyme," where the two words resonate more semantically than phonetically. George Murray's the only poet I know of who does it all the time – and it's not just a gimmick, as it complements the sort of metaphysical inquiries that go on in Murray's sonnets. This is a Shakespearean sonnet, in its thought-rhyme-scheme; just check it out if you don't believe me. What makes this particular poem work extra well is the degree to which Murray also uses his ear to structure the thing; note, especially, the internal slant rhyme – a chiming of both concept and consonant – of "dumb" and "dim" in line thirteen that set up so perfectly the self-deprecating pun on "dumber" in the fourteenth. That instinct for the consubstantiality of sound and sense, combined with Murray's handling of the conceit, make this a virtuoso performance.

Karen Solie, "Trust Me": In this mostly-free sonnet, Solie creates a surrealistic mood of urban alienation and despair with halting syntax and imperatives. Between octave (indoors/asleep) and sestet (outdoors/awake), the subject (not quite a speaker) gets up and goes about her business. Seemingly routine decisions take on strange significance, which becomes clear in the final line, as the first end-rhyme appears and induces a shudder of realization. Very sneaky, as readers of Solie's casual, polished poems have come to expect.

A.M. Klein, "Sennet from Gheel": Klein was, among other things, a scholar of Joyce, and this bizarre poem showcases him at his most Joycean. What might seem like sheer nonsense is actually brilliantly constructed wordplay. And if you know that Gheel is a Belgian town in which was located a huge lunatic asylum (or "lunasylum"), it becomes clear that Klein's linguistic jouissance is not merely purposeless play. Wait a minute, you say, this thing's only got thirteen lines! Well, yes, one brick short of a load . . .

Colleen Thibaudeau, "Nocturnal Visit to One Who Is a Chiropractor by Day": A surreal little bit of verbal voodoo, following the warped nocturnal logic of dreams. Irregular line lengths, end-rhymes falling where they may (note how "catch," echoed slantly by "watch," chimes semantically and sonically with the poem's last word), "écru lace" appearing first, literally, in the fifth line and then again, metaphorically, in the fifth-last line – a great deal going on here, the sum total of the details defying prosaic paraphrase.

Gwendolyn MacEwen, "The Discovery": Like most of MacEwen's poetry, this odd-rhymed free-verse sonnet is veiled in mystery and paradox. Who is this "she"? Ah, the land. Also an *ars poetica* or more basically a guide to fully-realized living: as soon as you think you've got something figured out, go deeper or go somewhere else. "The discovery" is more about means than ends.

John Newlove, "God Bless the Bear": John Newlove was a friend of my uncle's. Once, while visiting Prince Edward Island to give a reading, Newlove was tracked down by a young fan at my uncle's farmhouse. The poet, not surprisingly, was in pretty rough shape from the previous evening's excesses. When asked by his admirer if he wouldn't mind reciting a poem, Newlove looked blearily at the ephebe and croaked, "Gimme a dollar." Not sure what that has to do with this very moving free-verse sonnet, but it must be something.

Alan R. Wilson, "Orion the Hunter": An astronomical bit of politely politically incorrect wit! Like Diana Brebner, Wilson masks his stanzas by breaking them into couplets, but this is a pretty straightforward Petrarchan sonnet. It's one of a series of eighty-eight sonnets Wilson has written, one for each of the constellations. Good thing he didn't decide to do one for each star . . .

Richard Outram, "Remembrance of Betty E.": Richard Outram is one of the most brilliant and sadly under-appreciated poets going. This sonnet showcases many of his finest attributes. It's formally inventive, with its rollicking – expanded? – long line, each even-numbered line rhyming with all the others, the odd lines blank. It's wittily allusive, with the reference to the medieval lyric "Sumer is icumin in" followed swiftly by the reference to Bishop Ussher's crackpot creationist theory. The mix of high science with low diction is brilliant too, that "barrage balloon gone bonkers" and "boffins." Very smart and very funny, yet with a personal touch in that perfect punchline, bringing us back to the heretofore unexplained title.

Peter Sanger, "Fossil Fern": An unusual structure, four loose tercets (at least in terms of rhyme scheme; the individual lines are taut with repeated sounds) and a closing couplet, but Sanger's an unusual kind of poet. This sonnet could be taken as a statement of poetics for him, paying close attention to the details of things, particularly old things, lost and forgotten relics, and bringing them "back into green" with extremely precise artistry.

George McWhirter, "An Era of Easy Meat at Locarno": In case anyone thinks that references to Locarno and Jericho put us in foreign territory, these are actually the names of beaches near the University of British Columbia in Vancouver, where McWhirter taught for thirty-five years. The irreverent humour, goofy phrasing and the play of oddball rhyme-scheme and linebreaks are typical elements of McWhirter's work.

Peter Van Toorn, "Mountain Leaf": This is one of the craziest sonnets I've ever seen, which would perhaps explain the straitjacket it wears. As if the sonnet wasn't formally strict enough, Van Toorn invents a whole bunch of new restrictions to work against. The diction is Frostian in the extreme: the sonnet's 140 syllables are deployed in 123 words, only fifteen of which have more than one syllable (counting "tongue-tied" as a single word). It's the intricate patterns of repetition Van Toorn builds out of this sparse language that make this poem a dizzying bit of craftsmanship. Most obviously, this repetition takes the form of the identically rhymed couplets, an unusual strategy to see employed once in a poem, never mind seven consecutive times. This alone goes against all conventional workshop wisdom. But that's not all. Of the 123 total words Van Toorn uses, only twenty-three occur uniquely; the other one hundred are repetitions of thirty-two other words. Whole phrases ("a bird pushes"; "red roof") get recycled; and just look at the enjambments in lines three through six: "the more/it pushes"; "all curled up/in a cone." Interesting also to note the way in which the poem unfurls. In the first six lines, we find only two of the uniquely occurring words, whereas twenty-one appear in the following eight lines, giving the sense of a movement out of sheer neurotic repetition into more confidently purposeful – if still without obvious reason – activity, beyond the mere pushing of boundaries into the realm of art. Chief among the repetitions of single words is "push," which makes seven appearances; also notable is eight instances of words ending in "ound" (sound, round, ground). In a poem so intentionally and tightly structured, it can hardly be accidental that these specific re-iterations stand out: Van Toorn is pushing the limits of sense and sound, just as the bird is pushing the leaf across the roof, and likewise just for the sheer perverse pleasure of the labour, the end result of which, for both bird and poet, is a "stiff, crisp, bronze push."

Kevin Connolly, "Piano Gag": Connolly is influenced by surrealism, and this sonnet shows that the random associations of surrealist aesthetics do work well when paired with a non-random structure. A good move to break the formulae of the first two quatrains after the turn; a third stanza with the same syntactic structure would have been a bit much – and Connolly seems conscious of it with that rhetorical question of the purpose of his digression. It's hard to say why, exactly, but the couplet ties things up very neatly, doesn't it?

Lyle Neff, "Sleeping on the Weird Side": A kind of compacted *Notes from Underground*, this long-lined unrhymed sonnet, with its reiterated rhetorical "OK's" and "Fines" and "I knows" and its direct address of an unidentified "you," is a fine example of the form's embodiment of argument. And after all that rhetoric and all those ampersands, those last two syllables after the dash carry an unheralded weight of pathos.

Alfred G. Bailey, "Elm": Wow! what a dance of sound, semantics and syntax. Bailey inverts the old chestnut about the mindless innocent beauty of trees by the bold device of comparing the elm's root to a rat – a neat consonantal rhyme – a trick which has the dual effect of making us question our usual assumptions about trees and of exonerating the oft-benighted rodent. "Look well" he says, and he means it. The notion that a great beauty can be the result of bottomless appetite and chthonic formless energies is refreshingly pagan in its morality. And note how Bailey brings the sonnet back to the imagery of the opening in the closing couplet, forming a cycle.

Wayne Clifford: "*In which we are asked to assume a value for vivisection*": After twenty-six years of publishing silence, one-time Coach House Books acquisition editor Wayne Clifford re-appeared on the literary scene by publishing a strange and wonderful sequence of fifty-two sonnets, of which this is one. Like many of Clifford's sonnets, this one poses tough moral questions in a playful manner, pulling the reader in two directions at once. It's hard to get away with ending a sonnet on the word "love," but Clifford's remorseless eye leading up to the last line sanctions the gambit beautifully. Clifford is now in the process of publishing, in several volumes, an enormous sequence of over four hundred sonnets, making up for those decades of silence!

Matt Rader: "Electric Chair by Andy Warhol": With a light touch and dark humour, Rader's ekphrastic riff on Warhol's print of the Sing Sing electric chair makes the age-old connection between entertainment and commerce (doesn't it sound like an infomercial?) – and modern society's obsession with efficiency – and capital punishment.

Joe Denham: "The Sleeper in the Valley": This is a free adaptation of Artur Rimbaud's famous sonnet "Le Dormeur du Val." If you know the original, then Denham's title tips you off to what's coming, but the final two lines are still a wicked hit to the gut, in part because they do depart from Rimbaud's ending, but also because of the way Denham seamlessly works in the simile – but mostly because this ultimate act of self-violence is such a contrast to the placid, peaceful scene-painting that precedes it. And note how in those last two lines Denham slurs the sestet's two rhymes into slants, killing the sonnet's perfect form.

Barbara Nickel, "For Peter, My Cousin": Besides being a poet, Barbara Nickel is also a musician, whose love for music and fine-tuned ear come out in both the subject matter and form of many of her sonnets. Look how the hard-to-nail down pattern of rhymes and slant rhymes in the octave (I'd scheme it ABABBABA – and note how the two most radically slanted words are "pigs" and "ear" recalling popular idioms) resolves into a more definite pattern as the sonnet shifts from art to work and family obligations to the tragic inevitability of the closing couplet.

David Manicom, "Autumn Evening Sees Through the Blindness of Prayer": No matter how many times I read this sonnet, I can't quite figure out how Manicom did it and made it work. But he does, in a metaphysical manner that would have made John Donne proud.

Wilfrid Watson, "Tarquin": There's a terrific tension here between the relatively static shape of the rhyme scheme and the disintegrating frenzy of the syntax – more than a little like a house on fire. Watson's is a name you don't hear much these days – one of many such forgotten ones assembled in this anthology. I think he's worth another look, don't you?

John Reibetanz, "Rhoda": Reibetanz handles the controlling conceit of this subtly-rhymed sonnet with unobtrusive mastery. Note how the metaphors move from spacemen to the moon to the suggestion of menstruation and infertility foreshadowed by earlier references to seeds and barrenness.

Robyn Sarah, "On Closing the Apartment of My Grandparents of Blessed Memory": A gorgeously turned Italian sonnet. Notice how the octave's rhyme-scheme shifts, depending on if you read it "slantwise" (ABBAABBA) or by perfect rhymes (ABBCADDC). Talk about "lingering grace" and "the quiet that was like a sound." Notice also, especially in the octave, the subtle internal slant rhymes, particularly how "hand," "listened," "blond," "contained" and "wind" pick up the end-rhymes in lines 2, 3, 6 and 7. Another deft touch is the anadiplotic volta (yes, I've been looking for an excuse to say "anadiplotic volta"; look it up!), creating a formal representation of the speaker's wavering pause before the no-nonsense resolution of the last line.

Crispin Elsted, "Sonnet with Grammar Looking Over the Weald of Kent from Boughton Church": Elsted bypasses the usual bipartite asymmetry of the sonnet for a single syntactic onrush, structured symmetrically in a mirrored rhyme scheme. Quite unique. Another neat feature of this poem is the way the grammar breaks down progressively, an effect that mimes the visual blurring of land into haze in the distance experienced by the speaker "looking over the weald of Kent." Like he says "grammar is distance." In case you're wondering about the identity of Charles John Meade, don't bother looking. I did, and had no luck. And if you can't find it with Google, it probably doesn't exist, right? Well, I decided to get in touch with Elsted, who explained to me that he wrote this sonnet sitting on a memorial bench in the churchyard. When he got up and looked back, he saw that the bench was erected "in memory of Charles John Meade." Voilà! He had his last line and only had to make a small modification to the first line to get the rhymes to work.

D.C. Scott, "Watkwenies": Like most contemporary writers, Duncan Campbell Scott led a dual existence of dayjob and art. He made his living as an agent in the federal government's Department of Indian Affairs. Scott had a firsthand involvement in the suppression of the rites and customs of Native Canadians. All the evidence suggests that Scott believed in the rectitude of his and his government's actions, but a poem like this one, too complex to be read as propaganda, betrays a profound ambivalence.

David Hickey, "Preservation": An effortlessly informal sonnet, somewhat reminiscent of the style and subject matter of Don Coles, in loose couplets. Hickey roughens the rhyme and lets it slide when he needs to and avoids the potential pitfalls of sentimentality by focusing intently on particular details and letting them do the talking. There's a subtle irony in the final image that might be lost on readers not familiar with the Prince Edward Island shoreline. The dunes of PEI are held in place largely by the marram grass that grows on them. Walking on the dunes and uprooting the grass is strictly prohibited, as it damages the dunes' integrity and leads to severe erosion – dozens of yards have been chopped off parts of the PEI shore in the last few decades alone, making "tattered maps" a particularly apt metaphor. Hickey very deftly juxtaposes the careful preservation of the boys in their young innocence – by both the photograph and his poem – with their careless destruction of something adults go to great pains to preserve – which could lead to the very land they grew up on disappearing, even while the photograph and poem still exist, off-Island.

Peter Dale Scott, "Planh": A planh is a medieval funeral lament used by the troubadours; which is a very funny thing, when you contrast it with the loss the poet here laments. Scott, a world traveller as a diplomat, plays a similar joke with "arhat," meaning a Buddhist "worthy one." It all makes the sanctimonious claim of the couplet, preceded by a silly play on "earmarks," pretty hard to take seriously. A good lark on growing old gracelessly.

Evie Christie, "Old Men Sitting in Dizengoff Square at Night": Christie cheats a bit by using the title as the first line, but what the hell, she stretches a sentence over several lines so sweetly, I think we should forgive her. The turn comes after the tenth line, delayed enough to make what comes after doubly surprising. How this connection is made by the speaker isn't spelled out, but I think enough people have had similar leaps of consciousness that it doesn't need explaining. A gorgeous and, again, surprising touch comes at the end of the thirteenth line when rain exposes, not the remains of the bird, but the "us" that buried them. A deceptively complex poem and very sad, without being at all sappy.

Raymond Souster: "Young Girls": Souster isn't known as a formal poet, but this creepy Shakespearean sonnet demonstrates that he is amply able to rise to the challenges of the form. What I like about this piece is how completely unsentimental it is, while playing with the clichés of sentimental poetry on the same subject ("flowers whose fragrance hasn't sprung") – a powerful blend of innocence, malice and desire. He also handles diction and enjambments wonderfully, giving the poem the same sort of conversational ease as his more loosely structured free verse.

Elizabeth Bachinsky: "How to Bag Your Small Town Girl": Bachinsky's very good at – pardon the pun, please – marrying colloquial diction to the demands of formal verse; with slant rhymes and enjambment, you hardly know you're reading a sonnet at first. By such techniques and by moving the sonnet into the largely unexplored territory of small towns and trailer parks, she renovates it for renewed use on the topic of love. Like most good latter day sonneteers, she plays it fast and loose with meter, trusting her ear over the iambic metronome.

Suzanne Buffam, "Meanwhile": Damn near unparaphrasable, this poem takes a few readings for its sense to seep in, but the wonderful music of it makes those readings a welcome task. Like EE Cummings, Buffam upsets our linguistic expectations by turning language's connective tissues ("so," "but," "meanwhile") into main characters. Forgetting sense altogether – though what makes this an excellent poem is that Buffam doesn't go so far – the soundplay alone of things like "So felt the fingerbones inside me find/the fingered thing inside this foreign core" is outstanding. The intimacy she achieves through obliquity is masterful; there is something manifestly raw and urgent at the heart of all this polish and restraint.

Leonard Cohen, "You Have no Form": Leave it to Leonard Cohen to make a poem about nothing sexy. But it isn't really a poem about nothing; it's a poem about writing poems. Or not writing them. Or something. O Leonard!

Archibald Lampman, "Winter Evening": Lampman is perhaps the only Confederation Poet whose work doesn't require a great deal of academic special pleading to be appreciated. He was probably the best Canadian sonneteer of his day and this Petrarchan variant is one of his finest efforts in the form. This is not just brilliantly evocative description, but it also carries a depth-charge of emotional verity. Every bit as fresh now as it must have been when it was first published.

George Ellenbogen, "The Skaters": Very skillful how Ellenbogen, "tilting parallel" makes this poem about skating resonate also as a poem about art, or human activity more generally, in the face of the permanent blackness of death. A formally interesting piece, too, for the way Ellenbogen hybridizes English and Italian paradigms, slicing "wider rings" than either template alone would permit.

Ken Babstock, "First Lesson in Unpopular Mechanics": What anthology of Canadian sonnets would be complete without a hockey poem? Babstock, along with David O'Meara and Karen Solie, is at the forefront of a generation of Canadian poets blending gritty colloquial speech with sophisticated experiments in form and subject matter. The creative rhymes ("Messerschmitt/shit", "major/gauge or") of this modified Shakespearean sonnet provide structure that acts as a counterpoint to the free-wheeling approach Babstock takes to metre, with lines ranging from nine syllables to a whopping eighteen in the final line. Forget rules – for this sonneteer, it's all about flow.

Walid Bitar, "Tarzan": This sonnet is typical Bitar, a sceptic refusing to be held to a single stance, firmly committed to being firmly uncommitted, delighting in contradictions. A sharp reproach against the faux-sincere earnestness of so much poetry and against poets naively blind to the fact that sincerity in poetry is inseparable from skill in artifice. Notice how Bitar tightens up his rhymes in the last six lines, creating the lovely contradiction of statement and form – the looseness of quicksand vs. the solid platform of perfect rhyme – in the closing couplet.

Peter Norman, "Bolshevik Tennis!": A brilliant gem of wit, wordplay and controlled conceit. I especially love how Norman starts off with a challenge to Frost's dictum that writing free verse is like playing tennis without a net, only to serve and volley his way through a perfectly executed Shakespearean sonnet. A nice pair with Margaret Avison's sonnet "Tennis"; quite likely that Norman was consciously riffing off it, a return of her serve.

Milton Acorn, "The Completion of the Fiddle (N.M.)": It's a line shy of fourteen, making this poem a terrific example of what Acorn called the "jackpine sonnet," a form whose structure echoes the logic and sounds of an orthodox sonnet, but isn't bound to set patterns of syllable, stress, line and rhyme. Rather, like the tree for which it's named, the jackpine sonnet adapts its height and shape to the soil and weather in which it grows; it "can be a puny but tough battle-scarred veteran clinging to an impossible cliffside, or a proud giant in a pasture." It would seem that an awful lot of the sonneteers in this book have adopted the jackpine principle – whether they realize it or not! If you're wondering about the initials bracketed at the end of the title, this poem is the coda to Acorn's sonnet cycle, *Captain Neal MacDougal and the Naked Goddess*.

Robert Finch, "The Prunus": The mannered formality of Finch's poetry came under attack by John Sutherland for its excessive Englishness (ironic, Finch having been born in New York) in the 1940s. Finch didn't flinch, however, and continued to be elegantly unfashionable for another five decades. The sonnet was one of his favourite trend-bucking forms and this one, especially for something that describes a more-or-less static scene, really moves, with all the play of consonant and vowel Finch unleashes. Neat rhymes, too. He uses the four-stanza structure of the English sonnet, but the envelope rhyme of the Italian sonnet within each stanza, with the inner rhyme slant and the enveloping rhyme perfect.

P.K. Page, "Water and Marble": Is it a sonnet? Maybe not, but besides its line-count, something about its dialectical structure and the tension between the ephemeral (water) and eternal (marble) tells me it is. A tough, inimitable stunt to pull off a poem like this, but Page succeeds beautifully and memorably.

Richard Sanger, "Once of the Gang": A witty, ironic sonnet in couplets about the defeat of bohemian existentialism by bourgeois comfort. It might be only that if not for the mysterious "outsider," whose ghostly Camusian presence leaves us wondering just what isn't said here.

Adam Sol, "Sonnet with the Morning Paper": Just as it seems it's going to drift feebly to a banal conclusion, Sol's sonnet delivers a suckerpunch, reminding us that our domestic calm can be obliterated, just like that. By toying with the reader's expectations, Sol seems to be criticizing not only general North American complacency, but also the complacency of poets who write about the domestic while ignoring "stories of the world."

Gerry Gilbert, "Bannock": "Somplace new / & old" seems the perfect description of this stripped bare, disjunctive sonnet; "Bannock" nods not only to the sonnet tradition, but also to children's nursery rhymes. Eschewing complete sentences and leaping from stanza to stanza, Gilbert still manages to convey a great deal of imagery and mood in a mere 35 words.

Phyllis Webb, "Poetics Against the Angel of Death": Remarkable how many sonnets get written about not writing sonnets! In her play with rhyme scheme and line length, Webb shows there's more value in bending the rules than in chucking them altogether.

George Whipple, "Poetry": George Whipple is a sadly underrated poet, in large part because he tends to write understated little poems like this one. But what a gem! As if to say that each sonnet, like a snowflake, is unlike any other – recall Avison's "Snow" – he lets the rhymes fall where they may, all the while poking gentle fun at poets' self-importance.

143

Robert Allen, "Sonnet of Nothing": Go in fear of abstractions, said Pound. Well, you don't have to be an existentialist philosopher to know there's no abstraction so terrifying as "nothing," – unless it's "everything" – and Robert Allen's melancholic and melodic meditation on it does the alchemical magic of turning the abstract concrete. Part of what makes this poem so beautiful is its music. There's no regular pattern of rhyme, but Allen squeezes fourteen "ing" words into his fourteen lines, not counting "think" and "brink." He really makes much of nothing.

John Smith, "There Is One": Another unjustly neglected senior poet – the name doesn't help – Smith has been writing this sort of musical, metaphysical free verse for decades, mostly in this sort of loose sonnet form, or caudated versions of it. Like Wallace Stevens, Smith's prime preoccupation is with language and the inner workings of the human mind, which could be awfully dull as poetry if it weren't for him "getting it right" in lines like the last one in this poem with its string of hard stresses.

Index of Poets

Index of First Lines

Acknowledgements

Milton Acorn: "The Completion of the Fiddle (N.M.)" reprinted from *Captain Neal MacDougal and the Naked Goddess* (Ragweed Press, 1982) by permission of the author's estate.

Robert Allen: "Sonnet of Nothing" reprinted from *Matrix* (76) by permission of the author's estate.

George Amabile: "Poached Grilse" reprinted from *Rumours of Paradise/ Rumours of War* (McClelland & Stewart, 1995) by permission of the author.

Margaret Avison: "Snow" reprinted from *Always Now: Collected Poems* (The Porcupine's Quill, 2005) by permission of the publisher.

Ken Babstock: "First Lesson in Unpopular Mechanics" reprinted from *Mean* (House of Anansi Press, 1999) by permission of the publisher.

Elizabeth Bachinsky: "How to Bag Your Small Town Girl" reprinted from *Home of Sudden Service* (Nightwood Editions, 2006) by permission of the publisher.

Alfred G. Bailey: "Elm" reprinted from *Miramichi Lightning* (Goose Lane Editions, 1981) by permission of the author's estate.

Mike Barnes: "First Stab" reprinted from *A Thaw Foretold* (Biblioasis, 2006) by permission of the publisher.

John Barton: "Saint Joseph's Hospital, 1937" reprinted from *West of Darkness* (Buschek Books, 2006) by permission of the author.

Walid Bitar: "Tarzan" reprinted from *Bastardi Puri* (The Porcupine's Quill, 2005) by permission of the publisher.

J.D. Black: "Antiheroic Couplets" reprinted from *Black Velvet Elvis* (The Porcupine's Quill, 2006) by permission of the publisher.

Tim Bowling: "Pacific Sockeye, Moving East" reprinted from *Dying Scarlet* (Nightwood Editions, 1997) by permission of the publisher.

Diana Brebner: "What Is Homeless in Me, and Sightless" reprinted from *The Ishtar Gate: Last and Selected Poems* (McGill Queen's University Press, 2004) by permission of the author's estate.

Stephen Brockwell: "The Fruit Fly" reprinted from *Fruitfly Geographic* (ECW Press, 2004) by permission of the author.

Charles Bruce: "Early Morning Landing" reprinted from *The Mulgrave Road: Selected Poems of Charles Bruce* (Pottersfield Press, 1985).

Suzanne Buffam: "Meanwhile" reprinted from *Past Imperfect* (House of Anansi Press, 2005) by permission of the publisher.

Colin Carberry: "Abattoir" reprinted from *Ceasefire in Purgatory* (Luna Publications, 2007) by permission of the author.

Evie Christie: "Old Men Sitting in Dizengoff Square at Night" reprinted from *Gutted* (ECW Press, 2005) by permission of the author.

George Elliott Clarke: "Negation" reprinted from *Blue* (Raincoast Books, 2001) by permission of the author.

Wayne Clifford: "In which we are asked to assume a value for vivisection" reprinted from *On Abducting the 'Cello* (The Porcupine's Quill, 2004) by permission of the publisher.

Fred Cogswell: "Valley-Folk" reprinted from *The Stunted Strong* (Goose Lane Editions, 2005) by permission of the publisher.

Leonard Cohen: "You Have No Form" reprinted from *Stranger Music: Selected Poems & Songs* (McClelland & Stewart, 1994) by permission of the publisher.

Eric Cole: "Right Whale" reprinted from *Man & Beast* (Insomniac Press, 2005) by permission of the author.

Don Coles: "Sampling from a Dialogue" reprinted from *How We All Swiftly: The First Six Books* (Véhicule Press, 2005) by permission of the author.

Pino Coluccio: "The Time We Won the Cup in '82" reprinted from *First Comes Love* (Mansfield Press, 2005) by permission of the author.

Kevin Connolly: "Piano Gag" reprinted from *Revolver* (House of Anansi Press, 2008) by permission of the author.

Geoffrey Cook: "The next tide wipes away the muddy shoal" reprinted from *Postscript* (Véhicule Press, 2004) by permission of the publisher.

Mary Dalton: "Winter Coal" reprinted from *Merrybegot* (Véhicule Press, 2004) by permission of the publisher.

Joe Denham: "The Sleeper in the Valley" reprinted from *Flux* (Nightwood Editions, 2003) by permission of the publisher.

George Ellenbogen: "The Skaters" reprinted from *Along the Road from Eden* (Véhicule Press, 1989) by permission of the publisher.

Crispin Elsted: "Sonnet with Grammar Looking Over the Weald of Kent from Boughton Church" reprinted from *Climate and the Affections* (Sono Nis Press, 1996) by permission of the author.

Robert Finch: "The Prunus"; copyright holder not traced.

Prayer" reprinted from *The Older Graces* (Oolichan Books, 1997) by permission of the author.

Sharon McCartney: "Impending Death of the Cat" reprinted from *Against* (Frog Hollow Press, 2007) by permission of the author.

David W. McFadden: "Country Hotel in the Niagara Peninsula" reprinted from *Why Are You so Sad? Selected Poems* (Insomniac Press, 2007) by permission of the author.

Don McKay: "Stress, Shear, and Strain Theories of Failure" reprinted from *Strike/Slip* (McClelland & Stewart, 2006) by permission of the publisher.

George McWhirter: "An Era of Easy Meat at Locarno" reprinted from *The Incorrections* (Oolichan Books, 2007) by permission of the author.

George Murray: "Ditch" reprinted from *The Rush to Here* (Nightwood Editions, 2007) by permission of the publisher.

Lyle Neff: "Sleeping on the Weird Side" reprinted from *Full Magpie Dodge* (Anvil Press, 2000) by permission of the author.

Shane Neilson: "Rural Gothic" reprinted from *The Beaten-Down Elegies* (Frog Hollow Press, 2003) by permission of the author.

John Newlove: "God Bless the Bear" reprinted from *A Long Continual Argument: The Selected Poems of John Newlove* (Chaudière Books, 2007) by permission of the publisher.

Barbara Nickel: "For Peter, My Cousin" reprinted from *The Gladys Elegies* (Coteau Books, 1997) by permission of the author.

Peter Norman: "Bolshevik Tennis!" reprinted from *The Shape Inside* (The New Formalist, 2003) by permission of the author.

Alden Nowlan: "St. John River" reprinted from *Selected Poems* (House of Anansi Press, 1996) by permission of the publisher.

David O'Meara: "Postcard from Camus" reprinted from *Storm Still* (Carleton University Press, 1999) by permission of the author.

Eric Ormsby: "Childhood Pieties" reprinted from *Time's Covenant: Selected Poems* (Biblioasis, 2006) by permission of the publisher.

P.K. Page: "Water and Marble" reprinted from *The Hidden Room: Collected Poems* (The Porcupine's Quill, 1997) by permission of the publisher.

Michael Parr: "Palimpsest" reprinted from *The Green Fig Tree* (MacMillan of Canada, 1965); copyright holder not traced.

Molly Peacock: "The Lull" reprinted from *Cornucopia: New and Selected Poems* (WW Norton, 2002) by permission of the publisher.

E.J. Pratt: "The Ground Swell" reprinted from *Complete Poems* (University of Toronto Press, 1989).

Steven Price: "Rope:" reprinted from *Anatomy of Keys* (Brick Books, 2006) by permission of the author.

Matt Rader: "Electric Chair by Andy Warhol" reprinted from *Miraculous Hours* (Nightwood Editions, 2005) by permission of the publisher.

John Reibetanz: "Rhoda" reprinted from *Ashbourn* (Véhicule Press, 1986) by permission of the publisher.

Joe Rosenblatt & Catherine Owen: "Pounce" reprinted from *Prairie Fire* (27:4) by permission of the authors.

Stuart Ross: "The Children of Mary Crawl Back at Night" reprinted from *Hey, Crumbling Balcony! Poems New & Selected* (ECW Press, 2003) by permission of the author.

Peter Sanger: "Fossil Fern" reprinted from *Aiken Drum* (Gaspereau Press, 2006) by permission of the publisher.

Richard Sanger: "Once of the Gang" reprinted from *Shadow Cabinet* (Véhicule Press, 1997) by permission of the publisher.

Robyn Sarah: "On Closing the Apartment of My Grandparents of Blessed Memory" reprinted from *Questions About the Stars* (Brick Books, 1998) by permission of the author.

Peter Dale Scott: "Planh" reprinted from *Murmur of the Stars* (Véhicule Press, 1994) by permission of the publisher.

Goran Simić: "I Was a Fool" reprinted from *From Sarajevo, with Sorrow* (Biblioasis, 2005) by permission of the publisher.

A.J.M. Smith: "The Wisdom of Old Jelly Roll" reprinted from *Collected Poems* (Oxford UP, 1962) by permission of the author's estate.

John Smith: "There Is One" reprinted from *Midnight Found You Dancing* (Ragweed Press, 1986) by permission of the author.

Adam Sol: "Sonnet with the Morning Paper" reprinted from *Crowd of Sounds* (House of Anansi Press, 2003) by permission of the publisher.

Karen Solie: "Trust Me" reprinted from *Modern and Normal* (Brick Books, 2005) by permission of the publisher.

David Solway: "I'm writing this because I'm desperate." reprinted from *Modern Marriage* (Véhicule Press, 1987) by permission of the publisher.

Raymond Souster: "Young Girls" reprinted from *Collected Poems of Raymond Souster* (Oberon Press, 2001).

EDITOR'S POSTSCRIPT

Anthologies of this sort are a challenge for editors and publishers, particularly those working for a small independent press. With one hundred contributors, finite financial resources and no guarantee of good sales figures, production costs can be daunting, if not prohibitive. I anticipated running into difficulties with certain contributors (or their publishers and executors) asking for more money than the token amount we could afford to pay. I resigned myself in advance to the very real possibility that I'd have to let go a poem or two that I really wanted to keep in the book.

Though we have had to do a bit of bargaining, for the most part I've been pleasantly surprised by the generosity of spirit we've been shown. There is one poem, however, I was unable to include, and I wish it were otherwise. That poem is Elizabeth Bishop's simply titled "Sonnet." What stunned me is that it was not price that kept it from these pages. No, the publisher declined permission because Bishop "is considered an American poet and including her work in an all-Canadian anthology may cause some confusion."

I ran into this same thing in conversation once, when I told the editor of another anthology that I planned to include poems by Bishop and Lowry. This editor told me that she had intentionally left these poets out of her book because neither had ever held a Canadian passport. Well, as I point out in my introduction, one thing *this* book highlights is the cosmopolitan nature of its contributors and their chosen form, which is indifferent to arbitrarily imposed nationalities.

Including such poets as Bishop and Lowry (a Governor General's Award winner in 1961) is not exactly a bold subversion, either. Lowry's poems have been printed in more than one Canadian anthology and Bishop's appear in *Coastlines: The Poetry of Atlantic Canada*, published in 2002. But perhaps the most persuasive piece of evidence – outside of her poems – for Bishop's attachment to Canada is to be found in her Vassar graduation yearbook, in which she wrote under her own name, "Great Village, Nova Scotia." One needn't be a citizen of a place to call it home.

THE EDITOR

Zachariah Wells is the Reviews Editor for *Canadian Notes & Queries* and the author of *Unsettled*, a collection of poetry about Canada's Eastern Arctic, and *Anything But Hank!*, a verse story for children, co-written with Rachel Lebowitz and illustrated by Eric Orchard. Wells was born and raised on Prince Edward Island and has since lived in many parts of Canada, working in a variety of occupations in the transportation sector and as a freelance writer. He is also, sometimes, a sonneteer.

Marquis Book Printing Inc.

Québec, Canada
2008